# IRRESISTIBLE INTERN

## A COCKY HERO CLUB NOVEL

## ALIZA MANN

**Irresistible Intern:**
Edited by: Kate Marope; Jennifer Miller
Book Formatting: Jennifer Eaton
Cover Designer: DeliciousNightsDesigns.com

*To my dear friends who never gave me up, never let me down, never turned around, nor deserted me – no matter what came our way. To the Golden Brown Girls.*

# CHAPTER 1

## GENEVA CHAPMAN

*I* changed my clothes no less than fifty times that morning. Normally, I wouldn't have been so obsessive, but I wanted to make a good first impression. They are the most important thing, after all. Walking into a new job was hard enough. Going in as a new leader in a field dominated by men was something else.

The last thing to choose was heels, after an hour of putting on different shirts, skirts, and blazers, and making the stocking/no stocking decision. I had never been anyone's director of anything, let alone director of infrastructure. I mean, the nerve, when I'd been in the place as an intern only months prior.

I wanted to look strong, yet approachable. Smart, but still collaborative. Cute, but not too sexy. There was a whole thing that came with being curvy, and even more of a thing when working in a male-dominated field like IT security. Still, too much sexy and curvy could be called into question in a world where women were expected to manage men's desires. As woke as people were, they weren't *that* woke.

"Make the choice already," my sister, Leddie, yelled from the hallway.

She probably knew I was sitting on the edge of my bed, overthinking the height of my heels. "Fine. I'm coming." I didn't need to yell too hard for her to hear since we were living in a small two-bedroom in Jersey. "Did you eat breakfast? It's on the stove, probably cold by now since you insist on working through every damn meal."

I heard her grumbling but couldn't make it out. She was quite the grouchy-pants. I didn't care because nobody wanted to eat lumpy grits.

In the end, I went with a fave... my first pair of *truly* flesh-toned heels. They had been a gift to myself when I'd landed the job two weeks ago. I'd probably always known it would be that pair, even as I'd sat there procrastinating. I loved shoes, and while in college and taking care of my sister, Leddie the Grouch, after our parents died, money was always tight. But landing a job at Montague meant we wouldn't have to worry as much anymore. The pay was great. One day, we would probably be able to afford a house, post student loan debt. Hey, I was lucky to have found a job willing to give me a chance. It helped that I'd been an intern there during my last year of college.

I slipped my shoes on and headed for the living room. "Okay, how do I look?"

Once Leddie looked up at me, I turned slowly, already nervous about the black pencil skirt and button-down blouse with the deep brown belt that was a perfect match to my shoes.

"I like when you wear your hair down." She was still looking at the full ensemble as she spoke.

"You know I need to tame my curls. They're always a bit intimidating to people."

"Yeah, well, the bun is nice. And the pearls are a cute touch."

Instinctively, I clutched them with one hand, my other moving to my ear to make sure the matching studs were still in place. "You don't think it's too... like, fitted or something?"

"No. I don't. I think you look very... executive."

"That's great because I don't feel executive yet."

"You know what Dad said..."

"Yeah, yeah. Always step into your victory, and if you don't feel it, fake it. I remember very well, actually, but this is different. It's not high school."

"Girl, 'fake it 'til you make it' applies to every situation where you feel as if you're in over your head. And can you like... add some color? That red blazer will go nicely with all those muted tones."

I had to laugh. "I guess so." Shaking my head in her direction, I walked into the kitchen and peeked over the counter. "You haven't eaten, still. You know it's better for you to eat breakfast. You've got to keep your sugar levels balanced for your hypoglycemia. Eating later and later every day isn't going to help your cause."

"Fine, I'll eat. You are just like Mom, you know that?"

"I'll take that as a compliment. At least you have someone concerned about you. What a lonely world it would be if nobody cared." I walked back to the dining room and picked up my cross-body purse from the table, quickly rifling through it for my MetroCard, compact, tube of tinted lip balm, and mace.

By the time I was done, Leddie had maneuvered her wheelchair back to her space in front of the computer. While I preferred she consider not eating as she worked, I would be leaving in five minutes to be sure I was on time, and Leddie could and would do whatever she pleased. Getting her to take the plate in the first place was a major boon.

"Are you nervous?"

I glanced up at my sister. She was staring at me as she mixed her eggs and grits together. One of her grosser habits. I didn't like my food to touch at all, so just watching her raised my anxiety. Despite the egg thing, I could see she was genuinely concerned with how I felt in the moment.

"I am. But I think it's a good nervous. It's like there's this shiny goal I'm finally about to reach and I'm afraid someone will come and snatch it away from me. I guess I'm not afraid of the culture of the company or whether or not people will like me. I'm more afraid of failing. Of letting you down, and our parents, from wherever they may be watching over us."

Leddie set her plate on the table and stared at me even harder. "Gigi, come here and sit on the couch. I want to tell you something."

I did as she said, but I really didn't want her good vibes yet. I was content with the flutters in my gut and the random tingling of nerves. Fretting over things made them more real for me. Doesn't a person need that? If only to survive. It keeps everyone humble and thankful. I did it anyway, though.

"What?" I said.

"I know it's been hard, but at some point, you're going to have to stop being worried over things that are in the future or in the past. All that matters is the present. The present is yours to influence."

I was stunned to hear her make those statements.

"Aww. Thanks, Leddie. Now, where'd you get those quotes?"

She grabbed her chest and leaned backward, feigning insult. "Well, I never..."

"I think we both know that's a lie."

To that, we giggled another few seconds before I caught a glimpse of the time. "Shit, Leddie, I've got to go. Dammit."

I slung my keys into my purse. I decided in the last minute to accept her advice and add the blazer. She was right, after all. I had taken the monochromatic route. Maybe today, I would consider not being safe for once.

I practically sprinted back from my room. "All right, I left some sandwiches in the fridge for you to graze on for lunch, and I'll be home to make some dinner tonight. Oh, did you submit *Flowerville* to AppTech for that contest you told me about?"

"K, Mom. Yes, I already did that. I will be sure to eat actual food and not just energy drinks. Did you want me to be sure to clean my room tonight or..."

"Only if you clean *my* room." I didn't look back at her because it was as if I could hear her silent snark-glare as I grabbed my water bottle from the table.

"Hell, no. I don't have a hazmat suit."

"Pssh. It ain't that bad."

"Pretty sure you're just used to it. And Gigi..."

"Yup?" I stopped to look back at her, my hand on the doorknob of the front door.

"Be a badass. You're smarter than anyone there."

I had to blink hard to get rid of the tears stinging the corners of my eyes, the knot forming in my throat keeping me from replying. Instead, I just blew her a kiss and stepped into the hallway. I inhaled a deep breath before I took off for the elevator.

This was going to be the first day of the life I'd worked so hard for. Everything I wanted was at Montague Enterprises. I was ready. I just hoped they were ready for me.

## CHAPTER 2

### CALEB GREENE

*I* was no better than a caged animal waiting on my plane to taxi down the runway to the private hangar. Nas, my pilot, had just coasted to a stop, and I was up from my seat, waiting for the seal to release. I could hear him behind me as the cockpit door opened, and naturally, he was going to offer kind words. Not only had he been my pilot for years, but he was also a good friend. Too bad I wasn't in the mood for his overall jovialness.

"Yo, Caleb, you good, man?" he asked. The dude was built like a power forward and was barreling in my direction. He knew full well when a millionaire broke down somewhere, some photog was always, *always* waiting in the wings.

"Yeah, man. I'm good. Cali was just a bad scene, you know? I'm not in the mood for the speculation on my next move. Anyway, thanks for getting me here on such short notice. I... uh, I really appreciate it."

"No problem at all. I know you've had a tough run, so if you need anything else, just let me know. Anytime."

Nas extended his hand, and we dabbed one another up before the stewardess released the door. "I'm going to pray for you." He clutched the cross at his neck like he always did when he really meant something.

"See you soon." I could have told him I appreciated the prayers, that his friendship was needed during such a messed-up time, but I was anxious. Nothing was going to slow me down from getting out into the fresh air. The whole time we'd been flying, I'd envisioned my company going to shit. And it was killing me. Here's where I should have been longing to keep it, to ensure my life's work was secure, and I wasn't even sure whether I wanted it anymore. Freud could have used me as an extreme case example of ego at the moment, since I was mostly concerned that *he* didn't have it.

New York, however, was still New York. I could smell the sea-scented air, just like back home, but here, it was charged with the undying NYC tenacity and stagnant humidity. Everyone loved it. Once upon a time, I would have loved it too. Not today.

I made my way from the stairs onto the heated asphalt and found Dex's car and Sam the driver waiting for me near the hangar. I remembered the guy from the few times I'd been to see Dex and we'd hung out. Back before Dex had gone from the most eligible bachelor in the city to Mr. Happily Married. I didn't blame the guy. After all, he'd found his perfect woman. None of that was for me, but I was sincerely stoked for him. He deserved it. Hell, he probably needed it. Dex hadn't exactly been a sad sack before his girls had come along, but now, he was a proper husband and father, and you could see the positive change in him.

"Mr. Greene, welcome back to New York." Sam already held the door open, despite my reaching for it.

"Thank you. Glad to be back, Sam," I lied. I was just trying to be polite, but the words nearly scratched their way from my mouth, they were so far from the truth. The reason for my visit, different from my past trips aimed at debauchery, was to clear my head. My general lack of enthusiasm for my work shouldn't make me want to roll over for what was happening to me. *Who gets sued by a former partner?* Stupid-ass question.

Screw it. I just climbed into the back and didn't try any more small talk. I had fucking had it with the world. Most every modern-day tech god had been sued by a former colleague. Zuckerberg, Gates, fucking all of them. Christ... I laid my head back to close my eyes for a moment. It had been hours—maybe days?—since I'd slept. I felt like a freakin' wayward plastic bag caught on a tree limb, the mercy of a tiny branch the only thing keeping me from floating off the goddamn planet. Everything sucked.

"Would you like to go to the Waldorf first or Montague?"

"Nah, take me to Montague. Thanks." I tried real hard to make the period audible. I wasn't in a mood to talk, and the poor driver had done jack shit to feel my wrath. It wasn't his fault I was a dumbass. The only thing I could think of as I heard the partition slide into place between me and the front seat was whether or not I would be able to get out of my predicament, not whether or not I was being a dick to Sam. Dex had been kind enough to offer me refuge in his town, inviting me to come out for a couple of weeks away from all the shit. I must have been crazy—or desperate—to think I would be able to leave it all behind.

There I was... sitting in the splendor that was once— in what seemed like a distant memory—my favorite city, far away from the land of the Prius, yet unable to get my mind off impending doom. The worst part of it all was that I didn't have much outside of money. Okay, so lots of things come with money, but the excitement of app development and platform building was gone since I had people to do that now. The biggest part of the scenario was where did having people to do it leave me? I wasn't creating anything anymore. I was stagnant, like a pool of water with no filter. Did I really want to dive into all the murkiness below the surface and find out what was really bothering me? Probably not.

I needed to get myself together. The last article I'd read on the plane on the whole ugly sitch had sent me over the edge. Mostly because Blain Hoffman had shared my picture and intimate corporate details with *The Tech Times*. All the gory details were out there for the world to see. I'd seen that happen to giants before as well. And so goes the nature of giants, as we learned from nursery rhymes. Someone could always climb the beanstalk, steal your shit, then chop it all down. It was a handbook on how heroes were made, wasn't it?

The partition lowered, a gentle whirring that barged into my thoughts. "We're here, Mr. Greene," Sam called from up front.

Christ, how long had I been lying on the seat, mentally lambasting myself? The hour drive had felt like ten minutes or so. "Thanks."

"I can drop your luggage off at the hotel for you if you like. The doorman will have it delivered to your room."

"Oh." I glanced over at the weekender I'd haphazardly thrown in the car when I got in. "Yeah, that's a good idea. Thanks for that, Sam."

"Don't mention it. Mr. Truitt is expecting you. They have a security badge waiting for you at the front desk. You'll need to give the guard your name. Call whenever you're ready and I can retrieve you."

"Cool, thanks again." I practically rolled from the car, my anxiety stirring a little too close to the surface. I shut the door a bit too hard behind me, remnants of my pissed-off demeanor spilling over into my life. Per the usual.

The scent of Manhattan hit me as soon as I stood on the sidewalk watching the afternoon sun being reflected from the sparkling high-rise windows. The very air of New York carried weight and electricity. Everyone on the street milled about at top speed, and even the debris seemed to want to avoid contact. New York's vibrant energy was everywhere, but it was wildly different than Silicon Valley. Undeniably.

I made my way into the building and found the lobby full of... backpack-clad, fresh-faced techies. They were probably adults, but they looked like kids. Okay, maybe they just looked extremely young to me. Since it was before eight a.m., I hadn't expected it to be so crowded.

I beelined for the front desk, where, despite the mass of bodies, I received my badge within ten seconds. Dex's people were efficient, I'd give him that. I quickly headed for the elevator and watched as the state-of-the-art box made its way down. Once inside, I pressed for the thirty-second floor, waiting for the doors to close when, from nowhere, the most beautiful creature I'd ever seen stepped into my line of sight.

Damn, she was gorgeous. Her hair was a halo of lush

curls, her dark brown skin illuminated by shards of sunlight from the lobby windows. Her full lips, stained with red lipstick, coordinated with a chic blazer. I wanted to take in more of her, but the doors were closing.

I jumped forward, trying to stab at the buttons, but it was too late. She was gone, and I was left staring at sleek silver doors. And wasn't that just the type of month I'd been having?

The mystery girl was everything I liked, and, for the first time since I'd seen the article, I'd felt something other than anxiety or anger. A momentary reprieve just as extraordinary as the girl herself. But she was gone. Unfortunate because, given the opportunity, I would have asked her on a date. Now I was just as surly as I'd been before.

The elevator car moved me quickly, despite my earlier attempts to stop the damned thing, to my destination. Montague Enterprises was everything you'd expect it to be. The office teemed with staff as I stepped from the elevator. Across the expanse was a large glass desk with an older, redheaded Caucasian lady running the thing like a ship's captain. Things were being left there by people passing by, and the phones were ringing so much, it was like there was no such thing as online service desks. But maybe that was just how things went around here.

I sidled up to the desk and gave a smile to the receptionist, who didn't seem harried at all despite the bustling around her. "Hi there."

"Hi there. You must be Mr. Greene?" She smiled, coral lipstick and eyeshadow accenting her pleasant face.

"Yeah... how'd you know?" I asked, unable to keep the chuckle in.

"Oh, I make it a habit to familiarize myself with Mr. Truitt's guests."

"So, you Googled me?" No small feat, since I primarily avoided being the face of AppTech, allowing my fellow execs to handle all the media.

She merely smiled, and I knew I'd found her secret. "I'm Claudia, very nice to meet you. I can take you right into his office." She returned a comforting glance before placing a bag of carryout and a stack of mail on the countertop and removing her headset.

"You don't have to do that. I can find my way back. Just point me in the right direction."

"Oh, it's no trouble at all. Besides, it's kind of a maze on Executive Row."

"You don't say." I added the normally harmless tidbit of info to my arsenal of insults for Dex. 'Executive Row' would be right at the top the next time he drove me about in a smart car. "Thank you."

"No problem at all. Right this way."

She led me around the brightly lit workspace, and she hadn't been lying. There were lots of cube banks and hallways, all leading to a row of spaces with window walls overlooking the city. Finally, in the largest of the offices, I saw my old buddy.

And he saw me. From his smile alone, I knew he was poised to hurl an insult. The receptionist, seeing his door was open, merely waved me in with another of her warm smiles. I gave her a nod and entered, leveling him with a smirk.

"Caleb." Dex, wearing one of his signature suits, stood to greet me. "You need a lawsuit the size of Texas to get your ass to this side of the country or what? My company not good enough? Or is it my wife's cooking? Before you answer, I warn you the latter means no more boys' nights."

"Her cooking is the only thing that makes me want to come to visit your sorry ass," I hurled back. We met in the middle and gave one another a half bro hug. "It's good to see you, even if your hair is thinning."

"Fuck you, man." Dex chuckled before heading back to his seat. With a glance over his shoulder, he started in on the obvious—the reason I was there. "This shit is bananas. I never would have thought Blain would have played you like that."

"Me either... But before we get into that... There was a girl on the elevator... Well, not actually on the elevator because the door shut on her. She was gorgeous. Any way to find someone in this behemoth building of yours?"

"One girl out of a million? Oh, yeah. Let me just open my employee files for you. Man, get outta here. You'd need a department and employee ID for that kind of thing. I do want you to know, though... you should not be macking on ladies right now. Right now, you should be trying to figure a way out of this mess. Blain said you stole his idea then shut him out. I don't have to tell you— because fuck what the legal system says—the burden of proof is always on the guy with the expensive suit and private jet." He looked me up and down, once. Twice. "Well, one out of two, anyway."

I glanced down at my standard uni of a button-down and slacks. "Dude. And I contract that jet; I don't own it. My carbon footprint is the size of a pea." I strolled over to the window to take in the view of Manhattan.

"So you say," Dex quipped.

"Whatevs, man. By the way, be glad you don't have a use for your player's card anymore since you still say shit like *macking*."

"Daaammmnn, dude. Ease up. I wouldn't be advertising that pea thing, either, since you are still trying to use your card. And have a damn seat. You're making me nervous."

As I took what was proffered, I thought about his point for a second. There were indeed more pressing things to worry over. It wasn't the time for women—even if the mystery woman had looked like a goddess. "I don't know, man, I've gotta get this shit off my mind. At least for a second. We're in the discovery phase, but they think it's going to move pretty fast."

"You lawyered up?"

"Yeah. But my guy, Gangas Owenthal, warned me this is going to be a long, hard road."

"Shit, that's never good. In the interim, how can I help?"

"You already are. I need someone to talk this out with, and since the deposition will be here, it was perfect. Thanks for all this, by the way." I waved my hand in a circle to emphasize just him being a friend was enough.

"No problem. We'll see if we can't at least push that mess to the back burner. But for now, my legal team is ready to look things over. Give me your lawyer's phone number. They'll be a second on the case," Dex said, then grabbed a gold-plated pen from atop his closed laptop.

"I don't think I need that."

"Nah, bro. You need all the help you can get. Take it."

The warmth of gratitude heated in my chest. "Thanks, man." While I appreciated the gesture, I was reluctant as ever to accept anyone's help. Silicon Valley had trained me that help came with a price, which was silly since Dex was a man of honor in a world full of sharks. Any help he offered, I could trust was genuine. Old habits died hard, though.

"Don't mention it. And I hope you brought something nicer to wear than that. Tonight, we're going on the town."

"What is this? Junior prom?" I immediately wanted to rebuff his offer. I would probably just sad sack around, given my current existential crisis.

"Wiseass. You need to get your mind off your problem. I'm gonna help you do that."

After pondering for a few moments, I couldn't remember the last time I'd been out on the town. "Fine. I think that's probably what I need." And maybe getting back to my old self would be easier if I did some of the things I used to do, like carousing. I needed some time filled with friends and distractions. Somehow, though, my mind kept wandering back to the girl. The woman. And how I'd likely never see her again.

# CHAPTER 3

## GENEVA CHAPMAN

*S*hit, *shit...* I'd watched as the elevator doors closed smoothly, the scent of cologne wafting through the now shut gap. The dick—a handsome douche with deep brown skin and devilish eyes—might have smelled heavenly, but he'd clearly seen me trying to get on the elevator and done nothing. As a result of his jerkified behavior, I was going to be late for my first day on the job.

Alas, it wasn't his fault—at least, not *all* his fault. The subway had been slower than usual, and the streets crowded with a million tourists stopping and staring, as always when you're in a hurry. As my mother used to tell me, "You're on time if you're early," which was a quote from a guy with an unmemorable name. Sure, everything had gone wrong, but had I not worn high-heeled shoes like an idiot, I wouldn't have been in trouble.

Thankfully, it didn't take me very long to find the orientation room I'd been directed to from the employment package.

"Hello there," a young lady greeted me on approach. Man, she was fabulous. A blond with bright green eyes and a deep, yet feminine voice. We were dressed similarly, thankfully. The multiple wardrobe switches had apparently landed me on the right cultural fit. Yay, me. While I had been there previously as an intern, I'd worked on the IT help desk, and customer service was a whole different bag.

"You must be the new infrastructure director. Oh, wait, sorry, *director of infrastructure*. I'm the worst with titles, but a whiz at names. Ms. Chapman, right?"

I had to smile at her attention to detail. "Hi. Um, yes. Please, call me Geneva. Later than I wanted to be, thanks to the train, but I made it."

"Don't even worry about that. You're still five minutes early. I'm Alexis. Welcome to Montague."

"Well, early is on time, isn't it?" I shook my head, trying to ward off some of the awkwardness of the moment, and accepted the badge with a shaky hand. "And nice to meet you as well."

"So, I think most everyone is here." Her warm smile helped take some of the edge off. "Would you like some coffee or something before we begin the NEO?" She glanced at me as if to check whether I was tracking. "New Executive Orientation. I'm also bad with jargon."

Well, at least she had a good handle on improvement goals. And she was extremely perky. "Oh my gosh, yes. I was so preoccupied with getting here, I didn't have any this morning." My morning coffee routine wanted to hug the woman.

"I've got you. Sorry to say, it's most likely going to be a long day for you. You probably saw all the folks milling about downstairs. Those are the new interns. Lots of prep going on for them right now, so it'll be busier than usual. I'll take you to the breakroom, show you where the bathrooms are, then get you seated in the orientation. Right this way."

"Great. Thanks so much." I nodded and followed as she turned away. She led me down a hallway and then off to the left. The floor-to-ceiling windows gave a spectacular view of the city.

We made my coffee before she gave me a brief tour of the immediate area, then took me back to the conference room she'd mentioned. There was one long table in the center of the space and rows of chairs with about six other new employees waiting. I had never held a corporate position, but so far, everything seemed just like a normal job with new employees looking both petrified and thrilled.

"Here's where I leave you. And if you happen to need anything, just look for me."

"Will do, and thanks for everything." Once she was gone, I assessed the room, placing my coffee on the table in front of me and moving the waiting tablet and pen set away from the coffee. The last thing I needed would be to screw something up.

As I suspected, most of my colleagues were men. They were undoubtedly younger and richer than I was as well. They'd explained in the interview that Montague was branching out into IT Security instead of outsourcing it. No big surprise there, since it didn't make sense to outsource things when a company had greater control internally to make changes and less risk of breaches. I was set to oversee an infrastructure overhaul. It would be exciting, and I was to have a team, to be hired once I laid the groundwork.

I took a seat, arranging my purse and the folder I'd been given on my lap.

To keep myself from fidgeting, I extracted my phone

from my bag and scrolled through all the notifications. Since I didn't have my earbuds in, it wasn't the right time to listen to BTG, though their music always calmed me down for some reason. Instead, I opened *Flowerville* to play with my avatar. While I should have just been beta testing, I had to admit I'd become addicted. More than I could say for most games in the marketplace. My sister and her development team had done a very good job. One day, if I could, I would introduce her to a venture capitalist. Of course, that would be based on my ability to actually get in front of a VC group. All things in due time, though. I'd worked on the security patch myself.

The objective of the game was to get your avatar to their ultimate life goal—creating a life in *Flowerville* while revamping a dilapidated bed and breakfast an estranged aunt left them in a newly discovered will. Obviously, they would need to fall in love. My avatar had just made it to level ten—meeting the neighbor for lunch—and had fourteen thousand hearts to buy more materials. I needed twenty thousand to put the working fountain in the garden of my mansion.

When the neighbor—a small, pixelated image of a Black guy—appeared on screen, I immediately thought of the elevator guy. I selected the option to send him away, pushing Elevator Dude from my mind as well. I didn't need that mess on top of worry, and neither of them could lease any space in my mind. I was too focused on changing my life, after all. Good riddance to emotional clutter and all that.

"Hello, new Montague employees," I heard someone call.

Despite having to save a waitress from spilling her beverages, which would have given me fifty more hearts, I closed the app and put my phone away. "Good morning." My voice blended with the rest of the group.

When I looked up, I found a familiar face standing before us. It was my boss, who was easy to remember with his jovial appearance and bushy eyebrows. "I'm Cliff Griffith, Vice President of IT Security. My job today is to share our corporate culture and our organizational structure. But before I get to that, I can see we have some alumnae, so to speak, in the room. Ms. Geneva Chapman, one of our brightest and best interns."

For the entire time I'd been there, Cliff had been like that. I hadn't expected to see him during what I'd expected to be a routine intro to the organization. Somehow, that was comforting. Probably due to the distinct feeling of being an "other." Cliff didn't make me feel that, ever. I would be forever grateful to him.

I gave him a nod and a quick wave.

"Would you like to come up here? Maybe say a few words from your unique perspective of moving from entry-level employee to leadership at Montague? You do, after all, have the jump on these folks by understanding the culture."

White heat ran the length of my body, and I was sure my vision blurred for a minute. Panic. Sheer panic flooded me. "Oh...um... I hadn't expected to speak to—"

"I'm aware, and please pardon my departure from the agenda. Your story really is something. To go from intern to director is quite a leap. I think it's something that should be celebrated."

The round of applause took me aback. And simultaneously urged me from my seat. I gave a half smile and made my way to Cliff's side, smoothing my skirt as I turned around. "Well then, how can I say no? Hi everyone, and welcome to our first day. There will probably be a test after all this, so do take copious notes..."

A smattering of laughter littered the room. There were six people in there besides Cliff and me. Somehow, I probably would have been more comfortable with a hundred people. While it shouldn't have made any sense, I found crowds easy to get lost in. The more people gathered, the harder it is for someone to focus on the speaker. I'd practiced for this in the past and even done presentations in school, but the issue in this situation was that I'd been caught off guard. *Gah* times a million.

"So, I'm Geneva Chapman... um, which you already know. This is my first day in a leadership role. Ever. Just a few months ago, I was an intern here and it, like today, was one of the best times of my life. I have a love for technology, and as such, I'm aware of the inherent social responsibility of large organizations to protect the data of individuals and clients. It's the reason I chose the securities end of the industry. As you can imagine, I didn't grow up thinking *Oh my God, when I grow up, I'm going to protect data from online predators...*" A few people laughed out loud at that one.

"I was thinking *I want to create software and video games*. Then I discovered someone could steal a person's identity and ruin their lives through sloppy firewalls. And then I found out cybersecurity was a way to make a difference. I wanted in, which eventually led me here, to Montague."

I stopped for a moment, the urge to get into personal details on the tip of my tongue. Probably too much for the room to share my parents' deaths and that I had felt a responsibility to take care of my sister since I was eighteen. Or that it was *my* identity that had been stolen. Nope.

"So, I began coding for fun. When I shared what I'd been doing with one of my professors, he set me on a path that would change my life and perspective, ultimately leading me here. Getting accepted into an internship program from a company with such a strong reputation was just the tip of the iceberg. Once I got here, I learned so much more than real-world applications of C++ and SQL. I learned to work in fully integrated teams and, oh yeah, there was the bonus of leaders who encourage input. I knew in those six weeks I wanted to work here. It's rare that a person finds their forever job straight out of the gate, but from day one, Montague felt like home. Goodness, that sounds a little campy, but it's true. So... Cliff, is that what you had in mind?"

I turned to find him, and he was leaning on the table in the front of the room, his arms crossed, eyes squinted. For a moment, I thought I'd disappointed him, but then he started speaking. "You know what, Geneva..." He paused, so I nodded for him to proceed. "It's exactly what I want. So much so, would you mind telling our interns that during the afternoon break? I think it would be good for them to hear it as well."

Oh boy... "Um, sure." I flashed my smile and tried desperately to tamp down my enthusiasm. First day had been a win so far. I probably should have been a bit concerned that I was going to be speaking to yet another group of people about what was technically my old job, but was it a confidence boost? Hell, yeah. It most definitely was.

# CHAPTER 4

## CALEB GREENE

"*T*hat's all fine and good, but what is it that you want specifically? I mean, obviously, besides a great meal and some top-shelf drinking." Dex laughed. "You haven't exactly been yourself."

Legit question. But did I have the answer? I didn't know what I wanted. Maybe to exit the merry-go-round of topping other companies. Perhaps it was the feelings of inadequacy that came from nowhere with no sign of leaving. Or maybe, to stop all the damn toiling to no avail. Sure, I employed thousands of people who loved their jobs—I mean, they were an amazing group—but it all seemed to be for naught since the lawsuit.

"I don't know... It's absolutely exhausting talking about this shit. How about I get back to you, Dr. Dex? If I'd known I was gonna be psychoanalyzed, I would have been better prepared."

"I'm not asking you to lie down on a couch. Calm down, bro. I am asking you to figure out how to move on from here. Right now, you sound a lot like you're ready to pack up your shit and throw in the towel. It's not like you."

"All right, man. I think married life has you into talking and shit. What time do you get out of here? I'm starving." I shifted in my seat.

"It is literally ten a.m. I need to meet with new employees in a minute. Why don't you go down to the café and grab yourself some breakfast? You can also go poke around IT Security. I know how you love to get your hands in the dirt. I'll call over to the manager and get you a tour."

"Golly gee, won't that be swell."

Dex leaned forward and rested on both elbows, smirk ever-present. "You are one smartass fucker, you know that?"

"I do. Call your boy. I'll go meet him."

"Well, you won't have to go far. His office is right over there." As Dex pointed across the hall, his desk phone rang. "One sec," he said as he picked up the call. "Yeah?" After a brief pause on his end, he nodded. "That's fine. I'll go in and see them now." He hung up and stood. "Well, seems like you're off the hook for an obligatory office tour. I'm going into the orientation now because Cliff is taking one of them down to meet the interns. Some kind of welcome message to the people who made the cut. Shouldn't take too long. But go get something to eat downstairs. There a room right next to the deli. Big-ass nameplate that says Montague Executive Lounge. Can't miss it, and your badge works for that."

"Because, of course, you have a lounge. You're pretty old-school, Truitt."

This time he didn't smile. "You know my father. He's all about the affluence."

"Of course... All right, I'll see you after. Go get 'em, tiger. Show 'em who's boss."

Dex stepped around the desk, and I stood, following him out the door. I found my way back to the elevator from the maze and hit it down to the main lobby. After I stepped off into the atrium, I found a sign that read Enterprise Deli, and right next to it, a modest door that could have led anywhere. Figuring it was probably there, I made my way over. The area was packed wall to wall, and I almost didn't stop until...

Glancing over my shoulder, I saw... the mystery girl. She was positively beaming. Resplendent and, somehow, even more devastatingly attractive than earlier that morning. Someone was introducing her to those lucky people. Dex had said they were interns.

Naturally, I was stunned still. My feet didn't cooperate with my mind anymore, and my forward momentum was immediately halted. I wanted her.

Like I hadn't wanted anything in a good while. I drifted, quite literally, and fell into the crowd of backpack-clad young adults from earlier. We were virtually wearing the same clothes, so blending wasn't an immediate problem. Not that it would have deterred me. I could have been stark naked and would have stood there, flapping in the breeze for a moment to look at her. Breathtaking, she was.

"Hi everyone. I'm Geneva Chapman, and I'm a new director here, as of today." A round of clapping rolled through the crowd, myself included. "Thank you so much. What a warm welcome. I hadn't expected to speak to you today, but this is a pleasant surprise. I remember being in your exact position and wondering whether I was the badass coder I thought I was when removed from my isolated environment..."

My God, she was captivating as she glanced from person to person, connecting in a way I'd never been able to.

"...and placed in a room full of people who were on my exact same career track. The differences being I was older than most, I identify as female, and I am a Black woman. As most of you are at the end of your education in tech, STEM as a whole, frankly, you know there are minorities who are navigating the terrain. Women and individuals with different abilities and some minority groups can have increased barriers to entry. Whether you are in one of those groups or not, the road is hard and littered with obstacles." She moved the mic from one hand to the next, and I'd never been so jealous of an inanimate object.

"But I don't believe those are the only factors challenging individuals of all walks of life who seek jobs in Big Tech. There are so many others. Where we live is far from Silicon Valley, although no less expensive. Being an intern in one of these five boroughs is almost an impossibility. But look at you. You made it into one of the most competitive programs despite whatever individual challenges you may have faced. You should give yourselves a hand because you, my friends, are almost out of the wilderness.

"So, what's next? Well, once you make it through today, you'll be assigned a department within the information technology division, which could be anything from integration to dev to security. There, you'll receive a job assignment and the responsibility to create a project for presentation to your leader and possibly the C-suite employees, depending on how great it is, and looking at you, I can already tell they'll be amazing." Whistles and scattered clapping echoed throughout the atrium. "You won't be able to sleep tonight, and you will subsist on Red Bull and chocolate-covered coffee beans for the next six weeks in your efforts to shine your brand of magic."

Just for a moment, our eyes met. She paused, and I felt the sizzle between us—as if we were tethered by a cosmic event only affecting the pair of us. I held my breath for fear I would lose it. And then it was over. She turned away from me, refocused on her audience, and continued.

"But you will make it. You'll either secure a job at Montague, like me, or you'll go on to another organization anywhere in the world, solely based on the knowledge you gained while working here. And you will be magnificent. If I could impart any words of wisdom to you today, they are: one, give your one hundred percent best to everything you do here; two, cherish the relationships you'll build while working on your teams; and finally, have a blast. I don't want to bore you to tears, so I'll stop there. Does anyone have any questions before I go?"

I knew it was messed up, but I did it anyway. Unchecked and rogue in Dex's offices, I lifted my arm to the sky and hoped she would call on me. Three or four people beat me raising their hands and I could have cut them down at the stump. Thankfully, my impulse control was on ten, because I was tempted to walk to the front of the room and ask her out.

Every time she finished with one person's question, I would practically fist pump my hand in the sky.

"And you in the back..." she said, pointing in my direction with the mic, her eyes filled with expectation, my own personal captive audience.

In that moment, I had no idea what I wanted to ask. Shit... I searched for the best question I'd ever been asked by someone new to the field. "What's the most important lesson for new developers?"

It was almost as if I'd caught her unaware, and after a few blinks, she began. "The most important rule for developers is to beware who you meet on the way up. You never know who you'll see on your way back down." She gave me a sly smile, and I knew she was still pissed about the whole elevator thing.

While the questions went on, I stayed, hoping for a chance to speak to her after. Maybe I could apologize? I honestly hadn't meant it to happen. Finally, once the Q&A was done, the man she was with, Cliff, apparently, took over, and I saw Geneva head to the side and take a seat. Opportunity knocked.

I stalked over, using the breakfast buffet as a cover to make my way to her seat. I was behind her, watching as her elegant neck bent to stare at her phone.

In an instant, she jumped and turned to look at me. "Hey..."

I immediately held my hands up in surrender. "I'm sorry. I didn't mean to startle you. I actually just came over to apologize for not holding the elevator for you earlier this morning—that was my bad." I could feel the burn in my cheeks. Her vicious glare was so beguiling, my mouth went dry just looking at her.

She didn't respond right away. She just kept looking up at me, surveying my face, then glanced over the rest of me. "You can't just sneak up on a person like that." She rolled her eyes and laid her phone facedown on her lap.

She had a point. I stepped around her chair so that I no longer loomed over her. "I know, and I would have never done that. Charge it to my head. It's just... I recalled when you tried to get on the elevator with me earlier. That was messed up. I knew I had to come over and apologize. I didn't mean that or... or to give you a heart attack."

Her brows popped up at my words. "My father used to say that..."

"That he didn't mean to give you a heart attack?"

Her lips quirked and she rolled her eyes. I took this reaction to mean she was on the way to forgiveness. "No, man. He used to say charge it to my head, not my heart. I never heard anyone else use the phrase." When she was done, she smiled. I'd never been happier to make a woman smile.

"Well, now you've met me. He sounds like a smart man."

"That is probably a biased statement, but he really was. He's gone now."

"Oh, I'm sorry to hear that. Hard to lose a parent."

"Yeah... it is." I could see the sorrow in the way she bowed her head slightly and slowly nodded. I recognized it from my own past. For no good reason, I wanted to take up all the pain she'd ever felt and shield her from it. "I'm Geneva Chapman, by the way. But you already know that, don't you?"

"Yes, of course. Nice to meet you, Geneva. I'm..." *So, should I tell her who I am? Should I cop to commandeering a meeting just to talk to her?* It was a bad look. Maybe it would be nice to be someone else for a minute.

My life was an absolute shit show. A guy walking past with a hamburger in his hand offered the perfect solution. "Mac. I'm Mac Berger." I tried to look normal despite a wave of relief washing over me.

"Nice to meet you, Mac. Is that short for something?

Fuck! "Yup. Mac... Macaulay. Which is the reason I shorten it."

Recognition of the name finally sank in, as she blinked a few times, then smiled even brighter than before. "I used to love those movies. So, are you waiting to hear?"

"I'm sorry..." I honestly didn't know what she meant for a moment, so caught up in all the lies I'd told, her beauty, and the effects of the loose curls making a sort of halo around her face. She would probably be even more gorgeous with her hair splayed over my pillow.

"I gather you're an intern?"

What the fuck... Why had I lied? I could have whipped my own ass. Truth was, I didn't want anyone to know who I was because I wasn't ready to confront lawsuit questions. It was a hot topic in the tech world and the last thing I wanted to talk about randomly on the street. I needed a break. "Are you an intern?" I asked her.

She twisted her mouth, then bit into her lower lip to either stifle a laugh or make my dick jump out of my pants. I couldn't be sure, but there was no way she didn't know how sexy she was so the latter was probably true. "Maybe my little spiel wasn't as impactful as I thought. Must have put you straight to sleep. Remember the whole 'I'm a new director and today is my first day' bit?"

Nothing like putting your foot in your mouth. My attempt at small talk came out as just that—small. "My bad. I was honestly overwhelmed by the whole thing. Montague is kind of big-time, you know?"

"True. I remember my first time walking through those doors. I was a mess too. Anyway, we're on a half-hour break from orientation, so I thought I'd step away for a bit. Those iLearn courses are a killer."

"I bet." I didn't want to say too much because I had no clue what people did during orientations. I hadn't been in one since my college days. And back then, there weren't any iLearns. After that, I'd opened AppTech, so... best to shut the hell up on that topic. "So, which department are you over?"

"I'm in IT infrastructure, so I'll be building out the firewalls, integrity, and fortification, and mapping server use. You know, all that fun stuff. What internship are you after?"

I could have swallowed my tongue. "Oh, um... general IT."

"Yeah, but what's your specialty? I was an intern here not so long ago."

"Development. Hence my question earlier." At least I'd told one truth for all of my lies.

"Touché. Development, huh? That's what stole my sister's heart. The fun stuff."

"Yeah, it is... It's fun. But I'm more interested in what took you to the securities end? I would think you would want to do some of that fun stuff too."

There was that incredible smirk once more. She glanced around, and the room was still swimming with interns. "Well, I have a little more time. Won't you sit with me since you're waiting too? Doesn't look like the party is wrapping up anytime soon."

Damn, lucky break. Obviously, the lies had worked.

I'd just need to keep them up until it was time to leave town. Dex had suggested taking my mind off my problems for a few days—it may as well be in the company of a gorgeous girl.

"Don't mind if I do."

# CHAPTER 5

## GENEVA CHAPMAN

*S*hit, he was hot. I immediately wished I'd given him my nickname since he'd given me his. But, Gigi was a kiddie name, and I for sure didn't want him to think of me as anything other than a grown-ass woman. There was nothing about this gorgeous man I should be paying attention to. I needed to focus on what was important. It was my first day on the job, and I didn't want to get lost in being chummy with interns... How would that look to my colleagues?

As Mac walked closer to me, I noticed a few other things about him besides his handsome face. His sculpted body and taut shoulders, for one. Tech guys were usually a bit less than lean from all the hours on the computer and eating junk food. His skin looked warm, the deep brown coloring luminous, and his eyes were chocolate brown but lighter in the middle as the sun caught them.

He was tall, maybe six feet, and he didn't look like he was on an interview. He wore a cream-colored polo shirt and khaki slacks. He wasn't a slob by any stretch of the imagination, but everyone else wore suits. He obviously had no idea he would have to be twice as good as everyone else, as my mother used to warn me. And the last, perhaps most intriguing thing about him were those full, sexy lips. They were kissable. So very freaking kissable. Something else I wasn't supposed to notice.

"Tell me about yourself," I said. *Christ.* He even smelled good as he took the seat next to mine. A spicy, masculine scent, something like sandalwood and cloves, wafted over me as he sat back in his chair.

"Um, I'm from SoCal, originally from Detroit. I'm an Apple guy under protest, and I prefer old-school *GTA* to the newer versions." He lightly shrugged his shoulders.

"Ah, that's why I can't place your accent."

"Yeah, I know, kind of weird... It's a unique blend."

"It is... But hey, no room to judge. I'm from the Bronx, and well... you know. Pretty clear in my voice. No one ever has to guess where I'm from." Smooth—I was going straight into self-deprecation. "So, you went to school in Cali?"

"I did. USC."

"Oh, rich boy, huh?"

"Scholarship. Football..." He shifted in his seat. He was seriously the first person I'd encountered all morning who seemed the slightest bit nervous.

Somehow, it was comforting. No match for the surprise, though. I hadn't pictured him as a football player. Of course, I shouldn't have been picturing him at all. He was an employee. Not some random guy from one of my gaming rooms. I could legit end up in HR. "Football? Wow. Most of us never left our basements for all the coding. That must have been hard."

"It was all right. I was a bench warmer when studies conflicted... Damn..." Mac ran his fingers through his hair and gave me a surprised look. "I don't think I've ever shared that story with anyone. Maybe you should be a therapist." His smile was easy and lit his eyes.

"Hmm, maybe it's not too late. Probably need a second job to cover my student loans." I guess it was my turn for a bit of TMI.

"You wouldn't be alone."

"Ms. Chapman..." I heard from somewhere over his shoulder. I glanced around him and found Alexis from earlier giving me a friendly wave.

"Shoot, lost track of time. It was so nice to meet you, Mac."

"Nice to meet you as well, Geneva. Maybe we'll run into one another again."

"Yeah, I doubt they'll assign an intern to my staff, today being my first day on the job, but perhaps we will. Good luck to you."

I gave him one more awkward wave and walked around him. Naturally, I cut too close and our arms touched, an electric charge punctuating our connection. Oh boy, it was a good thing I wasn't working with him. Otherwise, I would have been in trouble.

CALEB GREENE

"Dex..." I barged into his office, hoping and praying his meetings were done.

He was on the phone. The look in his eyes told me I'd rushed in during something important, probably the meeting he'd mentioned earlier. At the moment, I didn't give a single fuck. Dex could naturally talk the white off a

Hanes T-shirt. "Tori, can I give you a call back? I'm sorry, something clearly involving a fatality has come up. Yeah, thanks." When he hung up, his eyes held pure malice. Again, I didn't give a fuck. "Caleb, I'm going to try asking this calmly and patiently, but what the ever-loving fuck would possess you to barge in here—"

"I need into your program. The girl from the elevator I was asking about earlier? She is incredible."

"You interrupted a meeting that dealt with Ms behind the dollar sign—not Ks, mind you—over a girl? Impulsive much?"

"Sometimes, you just know you need to see things through. My instincts make me who I am." I stopped for a moment, though. He was probably right. It did sound bizarre. It was one of the worst ideas I'd had in a while, but something about Geneva made me *feel*. I was nervous and excited while I talked to her. Somehow, even though I had every reason in the world to be closed off and cynical, she made me perk the fuck up after a long time of being half asleep in a cold, lonely world.

"I don't believe this."

"Do me this solid, Dex. I know. It's probably not the best idea I've come up with, and technically, I've lied about my name, but I need a win. Do this for me... I'll be gone in a couple of weeks, and we can forget all about this."

"Are you forgetting who you're talking to?" Of course, Dex had met Bianca through a similar situation, although he hadn't been pretending to be an intern... His had been an occupational change. And she hadn't been keen on him as a person based on some misgivings about rich people, but still...

"And if you had it to do all over again, would you?"

Dex stared at me for a good, long time. Probably about five seconds IRL, but it felt like a millennium passed. His eyes narrowed, probably resenting me for reminding him that the two most important people in the world came into his life based on that one moment in his past.

"I don't like it. Is she even an intern?"

"No, she's a director."

"Oh, hell no."

"I would think you'd been happy she's not some intern."

"Do you have any idea how this could be miscon-strued if it goes badly, intern or not?"

"How much can I fuck up in such a short period of time?"

"Remember Vegas back in 2012?"

"One time... it was once, and you're never going to let me forget it."

"It took me a month of detailing to get that shit out of my Porsche."

"I paid for it. Tell me you'll do it. I'll buy you a new Porsche."

"If you still have money from this fucking lawsuit."

"Oh, I'll have money. He's not including my subsidiary companies. Totally beside the point right now. Yes or no, Dex? You could be interrupting my future."

"You won't leave me with a mess on my hands?"

"No." I crossed a finger over my heart like a five-year-old.

"Promise me you won't ruin my company. Say it."

"I won't ruin your company, man. I swear on my own."

"Well, if you don't win, it would be worth shit, but I agree. On one condition."

"What's that?"

"You can't sleep with her."

"Excuse me?"

"You heard me. Don't sleep with her, because I'll feel like I allowed some predatory behavior to go on. And that, my friend, is the shit sexual harassment claims are built on."

"So... you want me to *not sleep with* the most beautiful woman I've ever met... Is that the ask?"

He didn't even answer. Just leaned back in his expensive leather chair and steepled his fingertips.

"Fine. I won't. But I'm pretty sure I'll regret agreeing to this."

"You could always come to your senses and go tell that woman the truth. You know, what normal people do when they meet someone."

"And how'd that work out for you in the beginning?"

"Fuck you, man. I had some extenuating circumstances going on."

"Uh-huh. How do I get my badge updated?"

"I'll text Cliff. He'll have it ready for you downstairs. Did you give her some dumbass name?"

"Macaulay Berger."

"You mean... like a MacBurger?"

"It was a push... I was in a tight sitch, man."

This look topped the last. I just held up my hand to let him know I didn't want to hear it.

"All right. Your funeral, man. Don't say I didn't warn the shit out of you."

I could have hugged him, but we were on the verge of a fight. I could feel it. And while he was being unreasonable about the sex thing, I could definitely see his point. "Thanks, for real." I could have thrown my keys in the air or some shit like one of those dudes in movies when they scored a big deal or something. I didn't have any keys, though. "You won't regret it." I turned to leave the room and before I could get out, he called me. "Yeah?"

"Don't you need to figure out how this will go down? Should she find out you're staying at the Waldorf, might be a deal killer."

"Shit, you're right."

"Fortunately, I have a bit of expertise in the area. Instead of going out tonight, wanna meet me at my house so we can hammer out your strategy? As you mentioned, I do have a bit of experience in this area. Not that I support this dumbass venture, but I don't want you to fall on your face, either."

"Spoken like a true friend."

Dex leaned back in his chair. "You know I'm going to put you in a really shitty place, right?"

"I wouldn't expect anything less."

"Serves you right. See you soon. Probably can't do lunch because I need to put this deal back together again."

"Text me. I'll head back to the hotel."

"Yeah, yeah. Get out."

Dex was shaking his head and wore a half smile when I left, which meant he was in. After our discussion, I was in a better mood than I'd been in in months. That should have been my first warning sign Dex was right—I was going overboard, like a kid with a new bestie on the block.

With that, I went back through the maze and bolted down to the first floor and right back to our spot. She had probably returned to her orientation by then, but I found myself looking for her.

Crazy thing was, I missed her already. Sure, we'd

been awkward together initially, but it was the first time in a long time I hadn't known what to say to a woman.

I pulled out my phone to check the time. Hopefully, Cliff wouldn't take too long.

"Mr. Greene." Speak of the devil. His voice was tipped in contempt, but I pressed forward.

Standing, I held out my hand to him. "Hey, man. I appreciate your help with this."

Cliff looked me over, disdain seeping from him. "I will do anything to support Montague, but as I expressed to Dex, I don't like this."

I tried hard to tamp down my immediate frustration. After all, he worked for Dex and was being dragged into things against his will. "Noted."

"Follow me. We'll take care of this down here so none of the other employees witness"—he gestured between the two of us—"this."

"All good. Thanks."

"The lounge," he said, turning on his heel.

I followed him into the room, and despite both Cliff's and Dex's opinions, I still couldn't keep my mind off her.

# CHAPTER 6

## GENEVA CHAPMAN

*I*t had been the day. First, I'd met the entire team, seen some of the most cutting-edge technology in the world, and had lunch with a few of my new colleagues. Between drafting my 30/60/90-day plan to implementation of the new information security platform and considering innovative ways to integrate the software systems at Montague, I was completely full. Excited, exhilarated, engaged, and so many other E-words. I loved it, and by the time I was seated in my office with the clock nearing quitting time, I was ready for the swanky leather chair.

I sat back, listening to the creaking sounds as it accepted my weight. Everything I'd worked hard for, everything I'd sacrificed, came down to my ass fitting into the Natuzzi leather and looking out over the fine wooden desk, the glass door wall, and the phone that would undoubtedly take me several days to figure out. I loved every bit of it.

Since no one was still in the office, I gave in to my inner child and spun around in the fabulous chair at top speed. Mid-spin, I held my arms out and let my body be carried away on the momentum. So freeing. The liberation of success seemed to propel my body faster. The room with all its bookshelves, glass, and counters whizzed by as me and my chair came to a slow stop.

If it were any other time, I wouldn't have cared, but to see the irresistible intern standing in my door watching me, I could have melted into the floor. "Shit!" I shouted the word and nearly leapt from the chair. Surely, the only thing grounding me was my fucking embarrassment. "How long have you... um, how long were you there?" Self-consciously, my hands went to my hair and I smoothed back the wayward strands.

"Not long. I think I got here near the descent. I take it you enjoyed your day?"

Not to be bested, I sat upright. "And I take it you're settled in after a wonderful day? Montague is quite a boon, so I hope you're taking full advantage of your experience."

"I am, thank you," he said, stepping inside. "May I come in?"

"Sure." I looked him over and found he a) was still hot AF, b) was a little older than one would expect an intern to be, and c) had a swagger that made my mouth go dry. "Come in and have a seat."

"Thank you... um... I don't know what I should call you. Madame Director, Ms. Chapman, or... I mean, since you *are* one of my bosses. What do you prefer?"

"Don't be silly. Geneva. Always Geneva. I don't want you to be stuffy with me. I'm not that person, anyway."

"Yup, you're right. Most people in tech are more down-to-earth than that... I mean, so I've heard."

"I honestly wouldn't know. I've been in tech for real

for all of ten minutes. And since I've only ever worked at Montague, my experience is even more limited."

"Well, I guess we'll find out."

I glanced over in his direction, trying hard not to stare at his big body as he folded himself into the chair across from me. "I'm sorry... I'm not following." Not a lie, but the actual reason I hadn't tracked him was because of how fine he was.

"I'm your new intern." The smile on his face was something to behold—a blend of innocence and mischief —and I had to wonder what made his eyes twinkle that way. "I guess you were wrong about them not giving you one so early."

"That doesn't... I'm sorry, not that I don't want an intern, but it's just that I'm new here and figuring everything out. It doesn't make a lot of sense."

"Well... we'll just have to figure it out together."

"I... I don't know what to say. Who assigned these interns?"

"I don't know, but in my orientation, Mr. Truitt handed out the assignments, so I'm assuming he made the choice?"

I could have swallowed my tongue. Dexter Truitt was the big boss. I'd never once met him in person, but all the employees knew who he was. A pang of jealousy snaked through me since that hadn't been my experience at all. But one thing hit me more than any other emotion. I would not fail at this first, unexpected assignment. "Okay. Well... guess I'd better get on board, then."

"Yup, we'd better. I just wanted to stop by and offer my services to you tonight... like, can I get you something?"

A flash of heat ran the length of my body. "Um, no... but I'll have some assignments for you by morning."

"Great. And I can give you my phone number... you know, in case you need something and think of it while we aren't in the office. Is that cool? I'm pretty um... accommodating..."

Now, the other comments, I wasn't sure about, but something about the last one made his intentions loud and clear. "So, Mac... just so we understand one another, I'm not someone who would um... fraternize with their intern. The boundary needs to be very clear here."

For a moment, it seemed as if my words didn't register, then, as his eyes grew wide, I knew he got it. Though, based on his reaction, maybe I'd gotten the idea that he was making an overture when he was just being accommodating. A panic alarm sounded in my mind.

"I, um... I'm sorry. I wasn't insinuating anything. I just meant I'm eager to get started. Service as in, I'll help with your projects and uh—"

"Oh, right. I mean, of course. I just know earlier we were a little flirty, and now you offered your phone number. So, oh God... I am so sorry. How stupid of m—"

"No, no, it's fine. I think I used some strange phrasing. I've never flexed my communication skills, so, my bad."

I released a deep breath and waved my hands between us. "Wait, wait. Let's just start again. Mac, I am happy you're my intern and come by here first thing in the morning. I want to start looking at the existing infrastructure, and we can review some of the coding. We'll come up with a project for you to give you maximum exposure and ensure you have the best internship. Sound good? I should give you my number in case you need to call out sick or... something. Give me your phone number."

"Yeah, boss lady. It actually sounds very good." He called out his number and I added it to my phone, then dialed his. "Cool. So, I'm gonna go ahead and take off for the night. Are you heading out? We can leave together if you want..."

"I'm was going to put some things away, but um... you have a wonderful night, Mac. See you bright and early tomorrow."

"Sounds like a plan. See you then," he said. He rose from the chair and headed to the door, giving me a wave before walking out.

I had lied. I was heading out, but hadn't I embarrassed myself enough for one night? Something about that guy made me lose all my cool points. And Mr. Truitt had made sure, in one coincidental decision, the next six weeks of the internship program would be the most difficult part of my employment.

"I'M HOME..."

The sound of the keys hitting the counter echoed through the entryway. Even before I stepped into the living room, I could hear my sister's fingers clicking away while working on her computer. Leddie was one who was always looking to find ways to improve anything she worked on. Everything from the mobility issues confronting paraplegics, to recreation, to being a better human being, and finally, to her app development.

I found Leddie hunched over her keyboard, her body leaning forward to allow her to get up close and personal with one of her four monitors. Onscreen, Leddie's avi changed into a flashy green maxi dress when she tapped on the closet door. Another of my favorite details.

*Flowerville* was getting rave reviews from the beta users already, but each and every suggestion was being vetted and tested, then proofed again before it was either discarded or added to the application. She most likely hadn't even heard me come in.

"Hello!" I was probably one octave away from yelling. At least it got her attention.

She glanced over her shoulder. "Hey, there. So, how did your first day go?" With a warm smile, Leddie turned her wheelchair and faced me. I could tell she was biting the inside of her cheek from the indentation. She always did that when she was nervous about something.

"Um..." I was teasing her, and she knew it. I twirled one of my curls around my fingers and rolled my eyes skyward, feigning apathy.

"Gigi... girl, you'd better tell me what happened!" Her eyes were wide with anticipation. I knew she wanted to know if I'd been greeted kindly or if there were office dynamics I hadn't been able to navigate—all those first-day jitters I'd shared with her. She wanted me to have a win.

And boy... didn't I need one. "Oh, nothing much. I just have one of those boss's offices they show on every single working-girl movie." Now my smile spread across my lips.

The slow smile began, making over her face that had been worried only moments before. She laughed aloud, moving herself in a circle in front of her desk, one arm in the air as she let out a triumphant *whoop*. "You're terrible, girl. I thought you were going to say you had a shitty day.

Tell me everything." Leddie patted the couch cushion once she made it over to it, and I obliged by practically skipping across the floor and sitting closest to her chair.

"It was awesome. I mean, there was so much to learn today, all these compliance trainings and history of the company, but I think I'm going to love it."

"That's so cool. I'm so happy for you. Now, can we celebrate?"

"I guess so. I just wanted to be sure it wasn't too good to be true, you know?"

"I do. But you don't have to be afraid anymore... we're gonna be all right. Because"—backing her chair up, she rocked back and forth, dancing in semicircles—"we're movin' on up... to the east side..." Her song echoed across the apartment we'd be moving out of sooner rather than later.

I joined in, remembering the show my parents used to watch on Nick at Nite, and mimicked the George Jefferson dance. "Movin' on up," I continued. We sang and danced for another few moments. Too often, there were so many worries and nothing at all to be silly about. We had bills and loneliness, heartache and sadness, all while the world never gave us a moment to be vulnerable, sad, or overwhelmed. So, the feeling we had together, the immutable joy at one simple thing, one goal to check off the list, carried us over into blissful territory.

I loved it. We danced until my legs hurt and her arms grew tired from popping wheelies over the laminate flooring. I collapsed onto the couch with one last audible sigh. "I have something else to tell you..."

Leddie backed her chair to the desk, not really paying attention to me, but listening still. "Um-hmm."

"I met a boy that was... distracting. Well, turns out

he's my intern." I sat up and scooted back into the cushions before shifting my legs onto the couch. Grabbing a cushion, I held the overstuffed bundle and clutched it to my chest.

My statement stopped Leddie's transition back into the land of the terabytes. "You what?"

"I was assigned an intern, and he's so cute, and, girl... I assumed he was flirting with me, and he wasn't. Oh, it was so embarrassing—"

"You did *what* now?"

I threw the pillow across the room, missing her completely due to my terrible aim. "I know, I'm an absolute idiot. Like, I completely mixed up the signals. Poor guy was just enthusiastic, and I assumed he was trying to holler at me."

"Well... first of all, if you ever went on a date, you'd know the difference between flirting and someone just being kind, so... I mean, you should probably start dating before you have to move to a nunnery."

"Harsh."

"Do you realize I've been on more dates than you in the last few months, and I'm not even trying to date?"

"I'm not ready to date. I just broke up with Tev—"

"You broke up with Tevin eighteen months ago. And good riddance. I'm not telling you to throw yourself at someone. You should, however, dip your clitoris in the dating pool."

I rolled my eyes and covered my face with my hands. I wasn't big on talking sex with others. Even my dear sister. "Ugh. So gross."

"Maybe. But I haven't told a lie yet."

I rolled my eyes at her and made a gagging gesture.

"Yeah, another thing besides your lady parts that's rusty—your comebacks."

"I'm going to make nachos," I countered. Standing from the couch, I stuck my tongue out at her before retreating into the kitchen and hiding away from her assertions. Before I pulled out the taco seasonings and started shredding the cheese—pre-shredded cheese, my ass—I heard her dive back into her grind on *Flowerville*.

Had it really been eighteen months? Still felt like yesterday. My heart was still swiss cheese, and I had more than a couple of open wounds left behind. At least, that's how it felt when I heard certain songs, smelled the woodsy scent of Tevin's cologne on some dude on the subway, or lay down in my bed with no one to hold me. Eighteen months since I'd buried myself into finding the right corporate fit and created change from almost nothing. And look where that had gotten me.

Everywhere.

No matter what Leddie said, I couldn't put myself through that again. I needed to focus on getting ahead so we actually could move on up. One day, anyway.

# CHAPTER 7

## CALEB GREENE

*I* arrived earlier than I should have at Dex's house. Fortunately, though, it was just the two of us, as I didn't want Bianca finding out about my web of lies and deceit. I took a seat at the table in their expansive living room.

"So, Macaulay, huh?

"Yeah, man. Shit's a mess, I know." I took a sip of whiskey, allowing it to slowly burn its way down my throat before continuing. "I don't know what I'm doing with her."

"That much is true. You sure you want to go down this path? I know you've got some issues to work out on the professional front, but this just seems like it'll add to it."

"I'm in it now. And you know I always see things through."

"Got that right. You don't have to do anything you don't want to, though. Like, should you decide to reinvent yourself... take a step back and figure out what you want." He swirled the liquid in his glass.

"How do you do that when people depend on you? What happens if Blain wins AppTech and I have to start over again?"

"Would that be so bad? Starting over?"

"When did you become this guy?" I leveled a hard stare in his direction.

In response, he guffawed. "I guess when I found my true north. I may not be right, but is it possible you're having an early midlife crisis? Kind of at odds with yourself?"

"Over what?"

"I don't know. Well—shouldn't you be telling me the answer to that question?"

"I'm good. I just need a minute. I'm going into mediation with Blain, and honestly, sometimes I wonder what I'm even fighting him on. I mean, for what?"

"Ego."

I shot another look in Dex's direction.

"What? Work hasn't exactly been a source of joy for you. Every time we talk, you mention retirement. Dude, you're in your late thirties."

"I'm thirty-six. Not late yet."

"I'm just saying. You should figure out if everything you're holding on to isn't just because you don't want someone to move your cheese."

I heard what he said, and while it had merit, that was not what I wanted to talk to him about. "We're off-topic. I need to look like an intern. You know? I haven't been a struggling kid in a long time."

"Yeah, Mr. Big-Time. But never fear. I have a place for you."

This was what I wanted. I sat forward on the sofa and set the glass down. "All right, lemme hear it."

"A warehouse."

"A what?" I managed to clamp my teeth down on the *"Oh, hell naw"* that threatened to bubble out.

"So, yeah... that's a warehouse with a loft in the building. It's pretty cool, actually. In two years, it's going to be luxury condos. You could say the cost is right since it's not completely done."

"You couldn't find an apartment somewhere?"

"On an intern's salary? Here? I would have had to put you in DC. Nah, this is good. It's not too bad."

"Is it... clean?"

"That's right. Forgot about your germaphobia." Dex's chuckle bounced from his vaulted ceilings.

"I don't like dirt. It's not a phobia."

"Whatever you say." He rolled his eyes and took a drink. "So, Sam will take you over there tomorrow. Need I remind you, this is not a bachelor pad. There's no hanky-panky for either of you. We have a deal."

"I swear, that's not what this is. I will come clean as soon as I handle the lawsuit, and if I decide to pursue her. I'm not into leading people on."

Dex narrowed his eyes in my direction.

"Normally. I just don't want anyone caught up in my mess. Besides, if Blain wins, suddenly, I'm a bad guy. No need having her happen across some article painting me as a big, bad villain. People don't empathize with rich people. And Blain is saying I blocked him from working in Silicon Valley, that I stopped his livelihood. Shit's kind of savage. I should be the one prosecuting him for slander."

"I think that's civil, but either way, I get your point."

"Anyway, I'd rather not have to get into intimate details on what happened and why with someone who may not even want a relationship with me. This is a distraction. And a chance for me to pursue the first woman who's interested me in a long time. Without actually pursuing her... get my meaning?"

"No. But okay. If that's what you want." Dex got up and took my empty glass, refilled it, and brought it back. "Next up, your internship. I don't have to tell you Cliff doesn't like this in any way. He's advised me that it opens up the company to risk. And dude ain't wrong."

I nodded, taking another drink. "This is good liquor, Dex."

"Thank you, but don't deflect."

"I know. But I told you earlier, I'm not going to sleep with her. I just want to get to know her without having all the other stuff come to light. When I understand who she is, I want her to see that I'm a good person before she can be tainted by whatever the hell they're writing about me."

"I hope this all works out, man. Seriously, this is a game of chance. So many things could go wrong."

"Well, if you see me, just remember to call me by my name."

"I don't think you'll have to worry about that. I'll rarely be in a room with you. It's Cliff you have to worry about. He's loyal, but he knows there's no way I would be able to legitimately discipline him for his treatment of a non-employee, so to speak." Dex held up air quotes to emphasize his point.

"I hear you."

"So... um, you think this is all worth it?"

I pondered his question. Dex and I gave each other shit all the time, but this was a serious question. It was one I should think about before replying. Geneva's face filled my mind, her bright smile, her welcoming personality, and her intelligent eyes were all things I could get used to. She was truly something—everything about her seemed to plug the gaping void in my chest. "Yeah... she's worth it."

Not just because Geneva was one of the most beautiful creatures I'd ever seen in my life.

*Sure, it isn't...*

I looked over at my friend. He had it all. A beautiful wife, a wonderful child, doing a job he loved... For the first time, I kind of envied that.

*Who the fuck are you, even?* The random thought was spot-on. I'd never even hastened a thought of the married life. One lawsuit and a lady I barely knew but was willing to put on a grand caper for had me questioning my life choices. Nah, I needed to get my shit together.

Guess that wouldn't happen anytime soon.

# CHAPTER 8

## GENEVA CHAPMAN

*Hopefully, day two will be better than day one.* I mean, everything was fine except I was having all kinds of naughty intern fantasies. The only thing I could deduce was my subconscious was a nasty-ass chick what with all the things I imagined doing to Mac. Damn my boss for saddling me up with someone so hot.

Despite my aversion to being attracted to one of my employees, I wore something extra spicy and left an extra button open on my oxford shirt. Granted, when I asked Leddie if I was too hot for the room, she laughed me out of the apartment.

Putting her giggles aside, I made it to work and sat at my desk, fighting off the urge to spin myself again. Once was enough. The login was new and took a few minutes, but before I could get into it, Cliff was back. He was my boss and a layer between Mr. Truitt and myself.

"Good morning, Geneva," he said, his voice a bit gruff. He was a taller white gentleman with sleek blond hair and obviously as nerdy as I was.

"Morning, how are you today?"

"Great, doing better than I deserve." He smiled, green eyes sparkling. "May I come in for a moment?"

"Sure, please." I slightly rose from my seat and extended a hand to the chair in front of my desk. "I was just getting in and don't have my coffeemaker set up yet, so I can't offer you anything."

"Oh, don't worry. I had my IV hooked up at seven this morning, so I should be jittery into the middle of next week. Much to my wife's chagrin, I am pushing a pot a day. Trust me, I'm fine." He took the seat proffered and leaned forward.

One look at Cliff and I knew he had something important to share with me. I could tell from the way his brows shifted. "So, I trust you met your intern yesterday? Mr. Berger?"

"Oh, Mac. Yup. He stopped by before taking off for the evening. I have to tell you, I was a bit surprised by having an intern assigned on the first day. That was... interesting. When I completed my internship, the program mentors were more senior employees."

"Yes, well... some of the rules have changed a bit. We opened up the pool based on the success of the program, so... I uh... I was as surprised as you. But I wanted to let you know, I'm not going to make any assessment of you based on your interactions with the intern. I will expect you to focus on your 30/60/90-day goals. He can just... work at your leisure. I have things for him to do should you require—"

"Oh, no. That's fine. He's fine," I replied, trying to keep the concern out of my voice. There's no way I wanted Mac to get shorted out of the experience because I was a newbie. "I think I can find something for him. He can serve as my admin and help me with reporting or do some system analysis and server integrity testing. I have plenty of work to keep him going. Trust me, Cliff, he'll get every bit of an education with me as he would with any other leader in the organization."

Cliff's look of concern slowly morphed into a much better smile. "Okay, then. I just wanted to give you some leeway, but it sounds as if you already have a plan. I had my admin set some time up for us to meet a few times this week and next, just until you get the lay of the land. I don't want to leave you on an island, Geneva."

"Thank you. I certainly appreciate it. I'm sure I'll have questions."

"Well, that's what I'm here for. Just think of me as a guidepost for the next few weeks. And remember what I said. If it's too much for you with an intern, feel free to send him over and I'll give him plenty to work on." The scowl was back again. I honestly wasn't sure whether it was disdain or not, but it was the first time I'd seen any employee at Montague ever seem even the slightest bit bothered.

"Oh, we'll be fine." As nice as Cliff was, I honestly just wanted him to give Mac a break. He hadn't done anything wrong. The only thing I could think of was maybe he was a bit older than some other interns, but then again, so had I been.

"All right. Well, I'll let you get to it. And if you have any questions, hit me up."

"Will do. Have a great morning, Cliff."

Cliff stood, smoothed his jacket, and turned to leave the office. Before he could get out the door, the topic of our conversation arrived. I glanced down at my watch and saw it was still early for Mac to be there. Most interns came in around nine. *Must be another change.*

"Good morning," Mac said, his smile widening when he saw me. He honestly wasn't even looking at Cliff. He was wearing a white button-down that accentuated his shoulders and black slacks, sans tie. In his hands was a cup of coffee I was immediately jealous of.

"Morning," Cliff replied stiffly, even if he obviously wasn't the one being spoken to.

Mac gave him an awkward smile and skirted around him, heading straight for me. I was a bit put off at their interaction, but you know what, maybe it was one of those pissing contests men had at work. I mean... Cliff was obviously seasoned, and Mac was certainly no threat to his position, but who knew how men got down.

"Good morning, Mac. C'mon in," I offered as a distraction since Cliff was staring at the guy like he'd been offered some liver cheese and sauerkraut. Thankfully, Cliff only shook his head and continued his trek from my office. I'd have to figure out what was going on between the two of them another time. "Have a seat. I spent some time thinking up assignments for you last night and wanted to run them by you."

"Great." He extended his hand, offering me the cup of coffee. "That's for you."

I was taken aback by the gesture. He didn't even know if I drank coffee. "Oh, well, I appreciate this, but you don't have to get me coffee."

"No problem at all. I wanted to. First impressions and all..."

"Ah, thank you. I haven't had any since I left the house, so this is just what I need. But I still don't want you thinking you have to fetch things for me or be an errand boy. There are so many more important jobs for you. Cool?"

With a slow smile that nearly did me in, he gave me a nod. "I don't mind. I'm an early riser, so it was nothing. So, let's begin."

Both of us sat, and I immediately started jabbering away about all the things we would do, all my ideas of vulnerability analysis and penetration testing... Okay, I had to keep my mind on track whenever I thought of penetration. How fucking old was I, anyway? Fourteen? Mac was so extremely insightful, his ideas equivalent to someone with decades in tech. Shit, maybe Cliff did need to be concerned about his job. Hell, maybe I did too.

It was noon before I even realized we'd been talking for hours. "It is lunchtime," I said after glancing at the clock. "I am so sorry. We didn't take a break or anything."

"I'm fine. I don't need one. I'm honestly just enjoying listening to the way you think."

A heated blush started from my neck and worked its way up to my cheeks. I was going to have to get over myself. "Well, thank goodness. Because I am talking too much. Are you hungry? We can continue chatting at lunch. I remember eating alone here for my entire intern-ship stint. It was not fun."

"Yeah, I could eat."

The tip of his pink tongue wet his lower lip, and I just about fucking drooled. Holy moly, I was heading to HR. "Great," I replied in a voice that was too damn high. "Your desk is outside there, so if you want to get your laptop set up, we can leave in a few minutes." For real, I needed to regain some composure. I was too into his conversation. Too into him, since he was my employee.

"That's cool. Let me know when you're ready." Mac stood from his seat, and I was so thankful we were in a work environment, because if he had worn anything that gripped his ass tighter than those black slacks, I would have died on the spot.

"Will do." I smiled. At least my voice was under control. I tried hard to look away as he left the room, but I was only human after all.

After checking a few emails, which were really only several welcome messages, I smoothed my pencil skirt and went out to meet the hot intern. "Ready?"

"Always."

"There's a place I want to go to. It's so good."

I didn't wait for him to unfold himself from his chair and instead headed straight for the elevator. Thankfully, there were already people on it, and we weren't in the tight space alone. I took the opportunity of him standing in front of me to surreptitiously take him in. I slowly ran my eyes up his body, inhaling his scent of cloves and sandalwood, taking in every ounce of his masculine divine. Pure sensory overload. He was kind of the whole package. Handsome, and so far, he seemed nice. I was beginning to think there was no such thing in a single man. Jesus, hopefully he wasn't hiding an entire family somewhere.

*Chill. And stop thinking of him as a snack. Even if he is, he isn't my snack. He is my employee.*

"So, what restaurant were you thinking of?" Mac squinted in the sunlight, the bright sun illuminating his smooth mahogany skin.

"Just over here..." I gestured to the park a few blocks over, the primo of all primo lunch spots. It was the perfect place to people-watch. For the rest of our walk, we continued our tech talk, and I tried not to think of how well his pants fit. When we made it over, I gestured widely to the food trucks parked on the sidewalk.

"And here we are."

"You mean food trucks? Oh... I've, um... never eaten from one." And his face told on him—he obviously hadn't planned on eating from one anytime soon.

"You're from LA..."

"I lived in Palo Alto, not LA. We do have some... so I hear. They aren't really my thing, though."

"Oh... did you have a bad experience with them?"

"No... I mean, I guess I just always wondered where they use the bathroom in those things."

My laugh came out like half a hiccup and half a snort. "So, you don't *know* you don't like them. You're just a little chicken about it, huh?"

"I wouldn't say chicken."

"I would."

"No, I'm just pretty concerned about eating from a place where urine could be in jars."

"Are you for real?" I was pretty sure my eyebrows were touching from my concern over this issue when he wasn't even positive there was reason for alarm.

"I am... I mean, *you* can eat there."

"I want you to try a taco from Pepe's. And I promise it will change your life."

"That is doubtful."

Instead of responding, I gave him one sound to punctuate the topic. *"Buc-caw."*

"Not a chicken, I say again."

"Then try a taco. I swear, if you hate it, you'll never have to go to another food truck while working with me."

Mac stared at me for a moment, skepticism written all over his face. "Fine. I'll try some Pepe's. If I get salmonella, I'm giving you the doctor's bill."

"In all my years of eating Pepe's and Brenna's, I've

never seen a single person get ill. Stop being a worrywart."

"Fine. C'mon. You can order for me since I'm a newbie."

"Food truck virgin would be a more apt name."

"I can promise you, I ain't no virgin."

"I'm gonna pop your cherry..." The moment I sang the words, I knew they were inappropriate. His brow quirked, but he didn't say anything. "I mean, I'm gonna get you your first foodie experience. If I'm going to order for you, though, you're gonna have to trust the process. Is it a deal?"

"Honestly, whatever it takes for you to stop saying you're going to pop my cherry, so I guess it's a deal."

"Okay. I won't say it again. Just trust me. C'mon." I grabbed his hand and dragged him to the line at Pepe's. As soon as I got to the window, Jorge came into view. His wife, Angela, was in the back with her hands in a bowl of something that would probably taste fantastic. Every Monday, they brought out their food truck and parked it in different locations, so it was a treat to see them.

"Oh, hello there, Gigi." He walked over to the window and leaned forward onto his elbows. "You found me again."

"I did. You haven't been to Harlem in a while. You should come back. We miss you. And your tamales."

"Yeah, that's why I stay married to this woman. My Rosita is the best, huh? What can I get you today?"

"Well, I'm popping this one's food truck cherry, so what's the special today?"

Jorge gave me a wink before waving to Mac. "I see. Well, I'm glad you brought him here because we're the best in town," he said, smiling in Mac's direction. "Today, we have chicken pozole, but it's spicy. If you don't want something so hot, I can get some burrito egg rolls. They've been selling like crazy. You know, my father, Pepe, would have had a fit to see something like that on the menu, but I like to keep things fresh, you know? You can tell me what you think of them, huh?"

"Well, it sounds yummy. Let's have four of those. Two for each of us."

"Coming right up." Jorge typed in our order and pulled a ticket to place on the old-school spindle just to the left of the ordering space.

Before I could pay, Mac pulled out a billfold and placed a card into the slot of the reader. He turned his back to me as he put it in. I didn't take the bait and try to glance over his shoulder to see what he was hiding. It was tempting but not enough to violate his privacy.

"You didn't have to pay, Mac. I invited you here." Low key, I was almost embarrassed to accept the kindness. He was working for me, and I didn't want him to think he needed to keep buying me things.

"I'm sorry. It's a force of habit. My mom told me men should always pay, and even if you're my boss, it's hard to remember."

"I know, but it's probably not appropriate for me to have an intern buying things for me. The optics, you know..." As disappointed as he looked, it had to be said. I couldn't risk doing anything that would get me fired or even put me in a compromised position. When it was all said and done, I needed my job. Even if he was trying to be chivalrous.

"You're right. I promise I'll never buy you another thing."

I tried to lighten the mood with a smile, but I was suitably awkward in the moment as we walked to the back of the truck to wait for Angela to hand us our meals. I'd always felt uncomfortable with people doing nice things for me. In my experience, anytime anyone had done anything nice, they'd expected something in return. It was a trigger, and in Mac's case, completely unreasonable. He was a nice man. He was a good person with a good heart. While all of it was true, I wondered how long it would be before the other shoe dropped.

# CHAPTER 9

## CALEB GREENE

*I* gingerly unwrapped the silver foil on the thing Geneva had ordered for me. Rather, *Gigi* had offered me. I noted the nickname she'd never told me about. Made sense, since I was merely her intern.

I had to admit the scent was heavenly as I raised it to my mouth and... I could feel her eyes on me. "What?" She had a caught-the-canary grin of a cat on her face just waiting for me to take a bite.

"Nothing, I just can't wait to say I tol—"

"Don't do it. I haven't even eaten it yet, and you're gloating." I sank into it as she extended her hand out across the table in the universal gesture for "don't take my word for it..."

And it was like a little piece of glorious.

"Don't make me beg for it." Her eyes sparkled as she goaded me.

"Fine. It's pretty good." I took another bite because damned if I could help myself.

"You're trying to get me to believe you've had better anywhere on the planet? Well, unless you are in a

Mexican village where someone's *abuela* just made the tortillas from corn and picked the vine-ripened jalapeños from her garden, you have to give me my props, man."

"All right. I'll have to give that to you, especially since I don't have an *abuela* to call up and ask."

"Thank you." She unwrapped her own delicacy and dove in. We demolished our humble meal on a park table in the afternoon sun, and while it wasn't what I was used to, it was the best lunch date I'd had in a long time.

"So," she started when she was done with her food, "let's get down to brass tacks. The first thing we need to do is finalize a project for you, and I've been thinking maybe we could build a cybersecurity program to prevent digital access cards—"

"Excuse me?"

"Yeah, I was watching an exposé on it. It's quite fascinating. Security badges are quite vulnerable. If someone loses one, the entire office is basically defenseless. So, we implement two-factor authentication with a digital fingerprint and retinal scanner. It's a bit involved, but it would be a great thing for you to focus on throughout your internship."

Here I was, supposedly a world-class tech person, and I'd never once thought of that.

She stopped talking, biting her lower lip. "That's not too much for you, right? And you can tell me if I'm doing the most."

"No, actually, I think that is a brilliant idea."

"I don't know. I mean, I don't know what my budget is just yet, and I'm not even sure how it would work, but—"

"No... Dex would b—I mean, Mr. Truitt would probably love something like that."

Despite my trying to clean up my slip, I still caught a

furrow of her brow. I would have to be more careful. "I'm thinking an app that would scramble a code for everyone who enters. They would need to punch in a code before gaining access to the suites. Could work, right?"

For a moment, her eyes grew distant. It was almost as if I could see her brain turning over the idea. I made a ball out of the aluminum foil from my lunch and tossed it between my hands.

"Yeah, I mean maybe. It could work." She leaned forward, and I was close enough to smell her lilac and vanilla scent. If I didn't know better, I would have sworn we were on an island somewhere.

"I think we'd need to get more information on what system is in place now and stuff like that, but I think I could come up with something."

"Great. And if you have better ideas, please let me know."

"I absolutely will. Thanks for the opportunity."

"No problem at all. All right, Mac, tell me something about yourself I wouldn't find on your résumé. We don't really know much about one another. Might as well change that." She smiled in my direction before taking a sip of her drink.

"Hmm..." I struggled hard to find something innocuous and not too terribly telling. Thankfully, my youth as a slacker kid came in handy. "I once came in first place in a skateboard competition."

Her brows popped. Probably not as deep as she'd hoped, but that would have to be okay. "Oh, wow. I guess I didn't picture you on a skateboard."

"Right? I know. I was obviously fourteen years old, but sadly, that was one of the last times I was on my board. I broke my thumb, and my mother made me shift to something less dangerous. Like weightlifting. That one, I never left alone."

"Oh, that I can see." Her eyes went wide, as if she didn't mean to comment out loud.

I laughed it off. "I mean, I used to have more time to do it. These days, I've been busy." An understatement. For the last few months, I'd been fending off the sharks. Something else I had to withhold from her. "But don't think you're getting away that easy. What's something about you not on the corporate website in your bio?"

"Oh gosh... I should have been prepared for this. Let's see..." She sipped from her Styrofoam cup, her lips twisted in thought. "When I was a little girl, my father brought home a cat. I loved him so much, but turned out he was bringing the cat to my mother as a penance for losing the rent money and then lying about it. My mother was so angry when she found out, she took the cat to the humane society. I was devastated... no like, for real sad every day. Crying, the whole nine. We were thinking of getting another, but..." Geneva fell silent for a moment before starting again. "Then my little sister came along and it was over. She's allergic."

My chest hurt, more over her father's betrayal of his wife than her sister being allergic. Especially since the child was the one to suffer in the end. I never understood why some men failed to protect the women in their lives. "I'm very sorry that happened to you."

"Oh, it was a long time ago. Whatever, water under the bridge. But I know I have trust issues. To this day, every time I see one of those stories or hear about someone being betrayed by a man in their lives, my mind flips back to that. You know? I always say I'll never be in the situation my mom was in—being lied to and mistreated again and again, because whoever is in my life gets one chance to lie. That's it. That's all they have—one time."

"I... I can see how something like that would scar you." More like, her words were scarring me. My heart clenched as I thought of my own actions. The damage I could do if she ever found out.

"It's like things that you get over sometimes have residual effects on every part of your life. But, don't be so sad. It's nothing you've done. And I didn't say it for you to pity me. It's just things from the past. All good. Probably too heavy for lunch, huh?"

I must have looked truly guilty, which she mistook for empathy. What a shit person I was turning out to be. "No, I don't pity you. Our past shapes us, good or bad. It informs our decisions, makes us more determined, and it can really be the catalyst for everything we do. You've done well for yourself with grit and determination. You should be proud. I'm not pitying you. I just wish I was as strong as you are." Probably the truest thing I'd said to her all day. She had more dignity and ethics in her pinky finger than I had in my entire board of directors, even if you included me.

Geneva flushed, the red deepening the makeup already on her cheekbones. "You don't have to say that... but thank you." She looked away from me, shifting so I couldn't see any part of her face.

"You're welcome. And I mean it." I didn't know what else to say, and when she didn't turn back around, I fell silent and left her to her thoughts. I honestly didn't feel like I deserved to intrude.

We went on that way until the foot traffic thinned out a bit. Geneva casually looked down at her watch, then back up at me with a start. "Oh, Lord. We've been here over an hour. I'm so sorry. Not doing well with time management."

I pulled out my phone, never really being a watch guy, and found it was nearly two. "I guess we lost track of time, huh?"

"I'll say. I... I unfortunately need to get back."

"Yeah, me too. I am with my boss, but I don't want them to send out a search party."

"Good point." She laughed. "We'd better get going. I don't want to stay late. My sister needs dinner, so I have to leave on time."

"Is she really young or something?"

"No. Nothing like that. The stove is a bit too high for her chair, and left to her own devices, she'd just as soon eat cereal as a hot meal. She's a game app developer. She's paraplegic, so I like to help her out."

"I'm sorry. I didn't know." Insert foot in mouth now. Damn, I needed to learn how to control my reactions. Geneva had a talent for putting me at ease and making me forget I was supposed to be her intern. Not her boyfriend.

"Yeah, I don't really talk about it. It's not the first thing I think of when I think of her. It's just that she feels like having different abilities isn't anything to be sorry about, and I agree with her. She's pretty badass."

Heat rushed up my neck. I hadn't thought of it that way before. "She sounds badass. And thank you for sharing that. You know, most of the time, we can have a pretty abled thought process."

"She is very strong." A wide smile broke across her

71

face as if it came from that special place inside just for when a family member was incredible. "Anyway, I don't want to inconvenience her since I said I'd be home. When my parents were alive, we had this thing where we never knew when my father would be home. Drove my mom nuts. I think I've been a little hypersensitive to it since then."

"I can feel that. Did you want to call an Uber to get us to work faster?"

"Oh no, we can hoof it. It's fine."

"I mean, I don't want you to be stuck at work later."

Geneva worried her lip once more. *That simple action is going to be the death of me.* I could feel desire stirring in my gut. Maybe it was a little bit lower than gut level. "Thank you again, but we should be fine. They won't get mad at me for like months. Right now, I'm too new to get scolded," she said. She pushed a thatch of those luxe curls behind her ear, and I had to fight the urge to keep myself from doing the other side for her. It would have been too much, a hell of a lot too soon.

"You're welcome. I mean, most people wouldn't have shown me how to find the best food trucks. I would have never come here looking for food."

"Well, stick with me. I'll show you all the hidden treasures. Wait until I take you to Battery Park. Have you been before?"

"You know, now that I think about it, there is a little jazz spot down on that end. But honestly? I've never done a lot of sightseeing during my previous trips. The people I know here aren't really into it." That wasn't a lie. Most native New Yorkers hated tourists and the droves of shoppers and non-natives with their incessant stopping and starting. Omission technically wasn't a lie... right?

"I get that. I normally don't either. I just don't want you to go broke while you're here. Your entire check will go to rent and food. Where are you staying, since you're from out of town?"

This next part was definitely lies. Thankfully, I'd spared a few. "I've got a little space not far from here." Yeah, one I'd never been to before, but okay... let's go with that.

"Great. At least you won't have to cover transportation to and from."

Yeah, I was going to struggle with keeping my promises. Next step, get that warehouse lined up. Shit, Dex was going to be sick of me.

THANKFULLY, I'D HANDLED THE POSSIBLY uninhabitable industrial living sitch with Dex. It was only a matter of getting my ass there and getting things set up. Why was I going so far outside of my original plan of chilling out for a couple of weeks with a girl I'd just met? Maybe it was time to honestly look at the why behind it all. It wasn't for sex. I had plenty of that when I wanted it. And Dex would probably kill me if I violated the terms of our agreement. I had lots of reasons to focus on the issue at hand. What was it about her that drove me wild?

She was beautiful. She was incredibly talented. But that couldn't have been the motivation... Could it?

Or was I hiding from the existential crisis confronting me? Avoidance of the bigger question—did I want AppTech, or did I just not want Blain to have it?

I honestly had no idea. For some reason, though, I knew I wanted to spend time with Geneva. *Needed to...*

Something inside was drawing me to her. And I hardly even knew her. Aside from our day at the office and a texting session, I didn't know much about her. While lunch had been intimate, I thirsted for more about her. As greedy as it sounded, I wanted all of her. I yearned to know her innermost desires, what she liked to eat besides Mexican street food, and her favorite color.

Damn, I'd for sure gone off the deep end.

Sam was waiting for me after I checked out of the Waldorf. "Are you all set, sir?"

I wanted to tell him *"Hell no."* I was probably making a huge mistake with the whole endeavor. "Yes, thank you."

We made it all the way there without saying a word. I was trapped in my thoughts on what I was trying to accomplish. Dex had been right, though. The spot where the warehouse was located was incredible and would make a beautiful location for condos.

Sam lowered the partition. "Will you be needing anything further today?"

I opened the door and grabbed my bag, but he met me on the other side of the car anyway. He held the door as I stepped out onto the street. Heat beat down on me in the summer sun. "Nah, I should be able to take it from here. I'm going to move some stuff around, but it should be fine."

"Very good. I'll leave you to it then." Sam smiled at me before turning to head to the driver's side door.

He always struck me as someone who knew what he wanted. I envied that fact about him. Here he was, jovially driving a schmuck around all day. While I should have been on top of the world, he seemed happier.

Funny how that worked.

As the car pulled out of the parking lot, I headed back up to what would be my home for the next weeks. The elevator creaked to a stop in front of me and I got in, pulling a half door down around me. The whole building was warm from the early sun, and I thanked God the windows seemed to be operational. By the time I made it to the top of the building, my Yves Saint Laurent shirt stuck to every part of me. *Note to self... maybe pick up some clothes that aren't so pricey.* Suddenly, I had a lot to do before reporting to work the next day.

Dropping the bag on the floor, I took a good look around. There was exposed brick all around, and the space was probably about the size of a large office. Someone had set it up with a toaster oven, coffeepot, and dorm fridge. There was at least a bathroom connected to the area, and it didn't look terrible.

I immediately stalked to the windows to open them. Up on the fifth floor, which was the sum total number of levels in the place, a breeze was blowing through for a bit of relief.

The sofa bed turned out to be fair. From the plume of dust that rose around me as I had jostled the thing out, I knew I had to get new sheets, but that was to be expected.

I had a few hours to make the place look like it belonged to me. The room was about as nondescript a warehouse as there ever was.

I made a mad dash to Target—I couldn't have Natuzzi leather strewn through the place—and picked up some knickknacks that looked like they'd been bought by a struggling student and added the right flavor.

I surveyed the place once I was done. Not bad for an hour's worth of work, thanks to some rush ordering. Some of the dust had even disappeared as I'd moved things around.

But would Geneva buy it? If she were to ever come by, that was. I guessed big wishes were in order. Yeah... real big ones.

Now, I just had to get her there.

## CHAPTER 10

### GENEVA CHAPMAN

*A*h yes... he still looked just as good as the day before. I almost felt silly for the extra primping and special attention to my hair and nails. Silly because when the world had become rightly engaged in ensuring there wasn't sexual misconduct in workplaces, I'd never assumed I would be mentally toeing the line. The fact of the matter was I wanted him. Like, *for real* wanted him. The good thing was I needed my job more than I needed him in my bed, so I would not be acting on these impulses. Three days, and I was positively smitten, even thinking of him all night—while I made dinner, during my chats with Leddie, and unfortunately, whenever I touched myself. Unfortunate because I would never be able to have this man I worked with. Who was my subordinate. Thankfully, it was Friday. Perhaps the weekend would offer a momentary reprieve.

"What do you think?"

I blinked back to reality as Mac leaned over my shoulder, revealing all the various design flaws in the current software. It was incredible what he'd figured out in a day and a half. "This is brilliant." Yup, it was short and to the point, but honestly, I'd gotten caught up in whether his cologne was sandalwood or pine. I'd never had a problem like this before. Of course, I'd never met anyone like him before. He was beefier than my normal taste, but most of the guys I'd dated in the past had more brainpower than brawn. In Mac's case, he had both. I wasn't ready for it. Even as I thought it, I heard the words in Kevin Hart's voice. *"I wasn't ready..."*

"I can't believe the integrity issues here. Glad they hired you. They need a lot of help."

"I think they're aware. The new system integration will be um..." Great, my brain shorted just looking at him. The sun was coming through the window behind him, illuminating his mahogany skin, and I was lost to it. I was lost to him... *Focus, girl.* "I... they will be onboarding a companywide software soon, so hopefully, that will eliminate some of these issues."

To my relief, Mac headed around the desk and was no longer shrouding me in his heavenly scent. As if he could sense my lady wood, I moved closer to the table and straightened my desk calendar, tape dispenser, and paper clip cup as a distraction. Nothing got rid of lady wood like office supplies. As my hand lingered on the wireless mouse, I felt the heat of his gaze on my skin. I looked up to find him staring down at me.

"What?"

"Who are those guys?" A surprisingly elegant finger pointed at my mousepad.

"Oh, it's just..." Heat flooded me. Hell, I really was a teen around him. "Those guys are the best K-pop group around. I might have a tiny obsession with them. And I wanted at least something that wasn't so stuffy in my office. I don't think it's appropriate to plaster the wall with them, but I can probably get away with a mouse pad. Although, since you peeped my game, maybe I need to reconsider this décor a bit."

"What's their name?"

"BTG. They are for-real talented."

"Hmph... never heard of them."

"I honestly feel bad for you. That's tonight's homework. You have to go immerse yourself in the experience. One album and at least two videos. You can report back tomorrow."

"I don't know..." He leaned on my desk, and I was immediately envious of the wood. "I'm more of a jazz guy. You know, Coltrane, Thelonious Monk... that kind of stuff. You into jazz?"

"Not if I can help it. The wild swings make me a little queasy. I don't know if I'm explaining that right."

"Can you really say you've enjoyed a song if there's no crescendo? I love the highs and lows. Always have. In fact, that's what makes me love it. The breathless ride."

I could honestly listen to Mac all day. He had a way of putting things... "Guess I hadn't ever thought of it that way. So maybe that's my homework assignment too. I'll check out that Monk guy and report back tomorrow."

"Or we could go to a jazz club after work today."

"Oh... I don't know if that's appropriate."

"Ah, see, that's where you're wrong. This isn't a date. It's homework. If you go, I promise I'll listen to BCB or whatever tonight."

"It's BTG, sir. But on the jazz club, I don't think we should." My stomach contracted with the mix of excitement and dread. Could I trust myself alone with him? I was already completely disarmed by his cologne. One night of charm may prove to be too much.

"That's cool. But if you change your mind, let me know. My nights have been pretty boring lately. The people I know here are all married off now, so I'm free a lot."

He seemed so earnest. Maybe I was reading too much into it. Maybe he didn't like me... in that way. Still, better safe than sorry. "Okay. I'll do that. My sister usually has dinner with me, so it's short notice too," I said, backpedaling on the whole propriety thing.

"I understand. So listen. I know you have meetings for the majority of the day so I'll keep working on the system integrity. I also need to step away from my desk for a bit. It's some stuff for school. Is that okay?" His refreshing honesty was endearing. Besides, I could tell he was really interested in doing a good job, and I recalled being just as eager to do well when I was an intern.

"Oh yeah. Take your time. You have access to my calendar for just those purposes. You can at least know when I'm going to be away. Take whatever time you need."

"Thanks, and you can let me know about the club, boss lady."

Something deep inside me tightened at his nickname for me. If I was having this reaction to him, what would a night out with drinks do to me? I guess it was too late to get scared now. "Okay, I will let you know. And if you'll excuse me, I have a meeting with Cliff, so I'd better get over there." I stood up and followed him out of my office. I glanced back at him as I passed and found him giving me a friendly nod. I quickly turned away, heading down the hall. I tapped on the window once I reached Cliff's office.

"Knock knock," I said, announcing myself at his open door.

"Hi there. C'mon in, Geneva. I let the time get away from me. Please, sit at the table, and I'll just grab my things."

"Great." I headed to the small, round two-seater in the corner of his office and put my padfolio down, sitting as he came over.

"You don't use a laptop during meetings?" He sat down and put his coffee mug on one side, laptop on the other.

"No, actually. I can organize my thoughts better on paper. I guess I'm pretty old-school. You know, I have friends who haven't written anything down in years. They make me feel like a dinosaur."

"Oh, I can imagine. Try being older than forty in the tech world. They all think I'm a grandpa, but it's okay. It's like being in the car with teenagers. You don't know what they're talking about, yet you can't escape because you're their ride."

I had to laugh at that one. "I honestly felt that way throughout college because I started so late. Guess we have that in common."

"We do. Well, let's see those plans of yours. We'll need to get this integration underway sooner rather than later. Dex didn't want to start until we'd hired someone in your role, which makes sense. You're the expert, after all."

I don't know why that got my hackles up, but it did. "I prefer teams, though. You know, all the knowledge of systems is with people who worked with them. There's no way a newcomer can gain enough info to manage on their own. Expert or not." It seemed Cliff was a button-pusher. If so, it would be unfortunate, because we would have to work together closely, given our respective roles. He frowned a bit at my statement.

"Oh, I'm sure you can handle anything that comes your way... I um... I do want you to watch out for that Mac guy. He seems kind of slick to me."

There it was. I wasn't sure of his angle. Cliff hadn't seemed racist. I was very good at picking that out in a crowd. But something about Mac really pissed Cliff off. "While I appreciate your input, Mac has been nothing but a good worker. He has lots of ideas and is quite capable."

"I'm just telling you to watch your back with him is all. I'd hate to see you get caught in the middle of something with him. At least he's just an intern, so he probably won't be here longer than six weeks."

"Wow. How condescending. You know, you hired me from my internship."

"Yes, but everyone isn't the same. You were at the top of your class and outperformed every other intern. I know exactly where you came from."

"If that's the case, you should be willing to give everyone the benefit of the doubt." I'd actually had high hopes for Cliff. After meeting so many assholes in positions of power in school, I thought he would have been different.

"Oh, I am. But in his case, he'll have to earn it."

"I'm not sure what the expectation is, but—"

"I wouldn't advise becoming intimate with him. That's all. There, I've said it. I can breathe easy now. Conscience clear."

"What are you... You know what? Never mind, Cliff. I don't even want to know. With all due respect, though, as long as he's getting the job done, shouldn't that be enough?" I returned my attention to the work on the page and hoped that would end the conversation.

"So be it. But don't say I didn't warn you. My last word on the matter is... sometimes, people just aren't what they seem. Now, no more procrastinating."

We moved into reviewing the schematic I'd drafted and the top-down project plan for our ninety-day migration, which Mac would help me with, regardless of what Cliff thought.

By the time we were done, I was ready to gnaw my way out of Cliff's office if I had to. Thanks to that asshole, I'd changed my mind about a night out with Mac. He was a good person and nobody should be written off by someone just because of where they came from or someone's preconceived notions of who they were.

By the time I got back to my office, there was steel in my spine, my resolve set on *F-you, Cliff*. The audacity of him trying to chastise me over an employee... I wasn't even sure what he was thinking. About me or about Mac. It was as if he thought... could he have thought we would end up in bed together because we're the same race?

No... that couldn't be it... could it? Or perhaps it was just Mac he didn't trust?

Cliff and I had been fine during my internship. So, perhaps he had a hard time accepting Black men? The mere thought seared through me, galvanizing in my gut. I didn't care what people thought or did in their home lives, but work was to be a level playing field for everyone as long as I was employed there. And that would include having drinks with a colleague. Goddammit.

I strode up to Mac's desk with high octane, but he wasn't there. Since I was on ten, I was kind of glad. I glanced at my watch and saw it was nearly lunchtime. That's probably where he was.

I picked up a sticky note and left it on his monitor. I'd simply written: Find me when you're back. I hesitated for a moment as I went to walk away, but then decided to leave the note anyway. I turned around and kept on going. Somehow, I knew it would always be a problem to leave Mac behind.

# CHAPTER 11

## CALEB GREENE

*I* hadn't asked for the extra time off for fun—I needed to hurry to the deposition before they fined my ass. It wasn't as though I *wanted* to leave Geneva, but no matter how much I enjoyed her company or wanted to wait around for her next request, I couldn't afford to risk my case.

Yeah, I was playing her intern—an inexperienced pseudo-errand boy—just to get her attention. But these moments with her during the last few days had been some of the best in recent history. I'd never felt that for a woman. I could have spent years doing things for her, just to see her smile. *No time to consider what all these feelings mean.* I needed to kick it into high gear and put on my game face. I hustled to Dex's attorney's office, who had kindly agreed to allow my attorney use of the space, convinced I'd done more walking since I'd met Geneva than I had in all the time I'd been in Silicon Valley. I'd been testing out an autonomous vehicle before the whole lawsuit thing, so there wasn't a heck of a lot of need for a car of my own. I didn't mind, though. Not when it came to her.

Once I got to the tall building, I made it up the elevator and greeted a sleek-looking receptionist. She eyed me a couple of times before getting up and escorting me to the boardroom that reminded me of Montague's. Corporate America loved glass. The whole thing smelled like pretentiousness and lemon-scented wood cleaner. It immediately put me on guard. The last time, I couldn't be sure since I was a kid, but the scent reminded me of my mother and her Saturday morning cleaning sessions. I pushed the nostalgic thoughts from my mind. I needed to focus.

My nemesis, Daniel Blain, was in the room via Zoom surrounded by lawyers who eyed me like a steak. I could tell they were ready to take every dime I had, if possible. They were most likely more than a bit pissed that I'd flown off to New York. I'd decided to take my trip despite the start of mediation. Owenthal had come to New York as well and honestly didn't care, since I paid all his billable hours and travel expenses.

Blain and I were like night and day. I was dressed in my self-imposed uni of black slacks and a button-down while he was wearing something I'd noticed in a magazine. His jet-black hair was in one of the cool-dude haircuts conducive for man-buns, and he sported a full beard. He looked like the proverbial hipster and not the tech-savvy business partner I'd once had. We used to stay after hours just to play *League of Legends*, and here he was now, looking like he'd never seen a set of headphones with that updo he was sporting. Once upon a time, he would have been dressed like me. *Fake-ass douche.*

"Good afternoon, Mr. Greene. We were starting to

get worried about you," one of his lawyers, whose name escaped me, commented. They were all the same.

I glanced over at Owenthal, and he looked nearly as pissed off as I felt. I gave him a nod. "Yeah, well, traffic is a bitch. Let's get started. I honestly don't have all day." I really didn't. I needed to get back before Geneva was out of her meetings. I didn't want her to get suspicious.

"No matter. We're all here now. Let's just get started. As previously advised, these sessions are recorded and can be used in the court of law, Mr. Greene. I'll start the recording now unless you object." I gave him a cursory nod, then he pressed the button. "I'm Lester Maxwell, and this is my client, Daniel Blain. Please state your name and state of residence for the record."

"Caleb Turner Greene of California." I was annoyed already. I worked to hold in the groan, but I wasn't sure how much of this shit I could take.

"Thank you. Your legal representation, Gangas Owenthal, is here at the request of Judge Lawrence. So, unless there are questions, let's begin." I saw Blain nod onscreen in agreement. I couldn't tell if he was avoiding my glare or not. Hope the prick wasn't. "When did you and my client begin your business arrangement?"

Surely, he already knew? "In 2015, we founded AppTech as a joint business venture."

"And when did it end?"

"After your client decided to screw me over on a business opportunity by cutting a side deal with a competitor."

For the first time, my silent ex-partner focused in on me, his eyes on fire and shooting dagger blades in my direction. "That's a damn lie."

"Please, let's remain civil. Just state the facts, and we'll get to everyone's side of the story."

Like a child, Blain leaned back in his seat, arms crossed over his chest.

"Now then, was there ever any written policy on working for outside vendors or competitors while employed at AppTech?"

"There is now." I couldn't stop myself from grumbling.

"At the time, however... was there?"

"No. I wrote it and called it the Blain rule, so people could officially say, 'Don't be a dick and pull a Blain.'"

Maxwell let out a *harrumph*—to clear his throat, presumably. "So, it's safe to assume, at the time, there was no agreement in place preventing either of you from working with other vendors."

"No. There was a stipulation on intellectual property, and the software he created was made on my platforms. It was supported by our tech. If he hadn't used our systems, it's safe to say there would have been no ability to produce the software. The data and software he shared belong to AppTech. Not him, and not me."

Maxwell got to scribbling on a legal pad, the noise of the pencil setting my teeth on edge. That was him for the better part of the deposition, firing off questions, scribbling in his notepad, and playing ref for me and Blain. It was enough to make me insane. By the time the two hours were up, I was grumpy as hell and ready to take my anger out on whoever wanted to catch these hands.

Once Owenthal told me what to expect in the coming days, I practically exploded from the building on my way back to Montague. I pulled my cell out, ready to call the asshole and curse Blain into oblivion. The only thing preventing me was the warning from my lawyer. No communication—a gravitas condition.

Instead, I made it back to my desk outside Geneva's office in time to see her coming around the corner. She appeared to be absolutely seething, her stride quick and stilted. She nearly barreled down an admin, and while she apologized, I could tell she was pissed.

Despite her demeanor, her smoldering look shot straight to my lower region. *Damn, she is hot.* "You okay?" I mouthed as she neared my desk.

"No, but I will be. What time will you be done today?"

"Um, whenever you need me to be."

"Five. We're going to the jazz club, after all."

I DIDN'T KNOW WHAT HAPPENED AND WHO WAS responsible, but I could have kissed whoever it was.

"READY?" SHE WAS EVERYTHING I LIKED. ALL EBONY skin, dangerous curves, curly hair, and so tuned in to everyone else's frequency to know how to be kind. Well, normally, she was bubbly and light—open and engaged to my closed-off demeanor—but today, she was passionate and direct, offering a glimpse of what might actually lie beneath her work persona. It was a nice change from the snark and pretentiousness of the tech gods I'd become accustomed to back home.

"Actually, I am not. I just need to call Leddie and let

her know I'll be late. I had some meetings that ran over, so I didn't get to tell her earlier. Busy day today." I watched from the doorway of her office as she gave me a warm smile, reached for her phone, and tapped out a text.

I pulled out my own phone. "Okay. I'll get us an Uber."

Geneva waved a hand at me. "No. Nope, nope, nah. We are going to take the subway like normal people do. You know? The most efficient transportation system on the eastern seaboard? That's how we're going. Just tell me where and I'll get you to it. Right after this call." She was dialing a number and speaking before I could refute her.

I hated subways and, for the most part, any area where there were more germs than people. I'd seen enough films on outbreaks to know that shit wasn't safe without covering your entire body in plastic wrap and sitting in a car all by yourself. I was already shaking my head when she hung up the phone. "That's not a good journey for me, so..."

"Listen, the subway keeps us from spending thousands a year in parking and gas and waiting in hours of traffic. This is Manhattan, at rush hour. We'll be in the car at a premium rate depending on where you're trying to get to on this island. It'll be fine."

"I don't feel good about this..." There was something in her behavior that clued me in to the fact I was losing this argument. It was either sway her by telling her I was a raging germaphobe—which did nothing for a swagger I was attempting to rock—or ride the subway and drench myself in Purell after. Fuck.

"There isn't anything to worry about. I ride the subway all the time. Now, c'mon. We are doing the whole immersive homework thing. Where are we going?"

"I'm thinking Bird Song Jazz Café. It's near Battery Park."

"Cool. It'll take us about ten minutes from here." Geneva began prepping to leave, placed her phone in her purse, locked her laptop in her desk, then headed my way.

When I didn't move, she extended her hand to indicate I should get to stepping. Dammit, I'd lost the battle.

I grumbled, yet still somehow followed her out of the IT suite and made it down to the street level. We entered the subway tunnel near Montague, and, while I bought my ticket, she poked fun of me pouring the hand sanitizer she'd loaned me on my hands before and after using the machine. To make matters worse, I smelled like a peach pastry. With one round trip purchased and through the turnstile, we were on the platform and being assaulted by all the sights and heat of July in New York.

The whole time, Geneva was documenting my discomfort through a series of joint selfies and sending memes to my phone about unsanitary subways. If she hadn't been having such a good time, I probably would have snapped back. But I couldn't because her smile was like a thousand points of light. She dazzled me with her overt ease in every situation I'd seen her in. It was incredible. *She* was incredible.

As we ascended from of the subway, I pulled out the trusty peach-scented hand sanitizer and slathered it on my hands before passing it back to Geneva. When she didn't take it, I called her attention to the matter. "Want some?"

"Yeah. But this doesn't mean the subway is any dirtier than any other place in the city." When she was done, she slipped it back into her brown leather crossbody.

"I'm finding this oddly discomforting. Was that the goal or..."

"You have a lot of hang-ups."

"I just know better than to assume I'm safe from ages-old bacteria."

"Pretty sure I have T-cell immunity from riding the subway. Now, where's this Bird Song's?"

"It's on the waterfront... based on the map." I opened my phone again. I didn't remember the exact street, and I'd never gone there on foot, so I was properly lost. I tilted the phone in her direction so she could see our recommended route.

"Oh, I know where that is. But let's take the long way. It'll give you a chance to sightsee. You game for a little adventure?"

"I thought that's what the trip on the subway was. That's enough for one day."

"C'mon. Live a little," was all she said before turning and walking away from me.

"You just gonna do me like that?" I held my hands out at my side, ready to make a grand gesture.

"Why yes. Yes, I am," she hollered over her shoulder and didn't stop her forward momentum, her hair bouncing with her flirtatious walk.

"Fine. I'm coming. Just know, I'm mentally protesting."

"Protest all you want when we're seated in our booth and drinking margaritas."

I don't know why I pretended I was able to resist her. The farther away she moved from me, the more I wanted her close. I took a quick jog to catch up and glanced over at her. She wore a self-satisfied smile, and I knew she'd won. Yet again.

It was a hot day, and my shirt was sticking to me. I missed the consistent seventy or so degrees back home. Somehow, though, the heat didn't bother me as much since I was preoccupied with her. She was something, and I would have followed her around like a puppy dog.

She'd already gotten me to abandon my common sense and get on the subway. And I'd only known her four days. I couldn't imagine what else she could manage if I stayed with her forever...

Pure crazy talk, and I knew it. It paid off, though. We traveled through a building with the stairs from *Bonfire of the Vanities*, and she got me to reluctantly snap a pic of her for one of her social media accounts. She was exasperated that I wasn't on any. After several assertions, where she accused me of being a Boomer, we arrived at Bird Song's. Amber, the hostess, took us back to our table. The restaurant wasn't wildly different from any other restaurant or bar in New York, but we had a view of the Hudson. I'd wanted somewhere that looked like a college kid could afford it, but it was way nicer than I'd remembered. Maybe because I was with Geneva.

Amber hurried back with two glasses of water and informed us who would be our waitperson for the evening. It didn't matter. Not to me anyway. I only cared about being there with Geneva.

"You must have lots of savings to afford these places, and calling car services left and right?" Even as she said the words, I could tell she hadn't meant them the way they sounded. She held her hand over her mouth and immediately shook her head. "I'm so sorry. I was supposed to say something like... hell, I don't know. Don't answer that. My God..."

I couldn't help but smile at her forwardness. "It's

okay. I just had some scholarships for school and then do some odd jobs. I also save by staying at the warehouse I live in. It's not exactly up to code. I don't pay rent right now and had some savings, so... I can do some things." In that moment, I wondered whether one consistent lie was better than a million tiny ones. Best to keep it simple, anyway. "So, I don't have a lot of money, but I won't have student loans."

"Man, I should have done something like that." Her look of suspicion transitioned to something like admiration. "I didn't have a lot of free time though... you know, my sister and her rehabilitation were pretty much a full-time job. She was injured in the same car crash that killed my parents. The spinal cord damage affected her legs, so it was a lot for her to get through. Then, when she started to get better and learned to navigate, I had a chance to focus on me."

"Your job was way more important. I slacked around for a lot of my early college years and had no idea of what I truly wanted to do until I was already developing random apps. I think I could have been a four-year grad instead of five if I'd only focused a bit more."

"I would have been a four-year grad if it didn't cost so much, so I guess we're even."

"We are. Quite. So, I'm going to order a drink tonight, I think. What about you—will you be having any libations?" I wiggled my brows at her.

She dissolved into a round of giggles. It's easy to tell when a woman is at ease because their ability to laugh at corny jokes increases by about a million. Lucky me. This girl was way out of my league with her brilliance and wit. Not to mention her beauty. I needed all the points I could garner. "Yes. I'll have a glass of wine. That's it, though, because two glasses is my true limit. Three and things get sloppy."

"Note to self: give Geneva three glasses of wine."

More laughter through my whiskey, her cab, and two courses, accompanied by the best music, which she even seemed to enjoy. I managed to talk her into dessert, because honestly, I didn't want the night to end. I wanted to kiss her, to pull her against my body as the world passed us by.

I held my position, though. I didn't want to hound dog her—take her out for drinks and press her for sex. I could wait. She was worth the courtship. Even though I allowed those thoughts, I knew I didn't have a lot of time. I was going to have to go back to my world soon. It was easy to see, after a night like this with Geneva, why I'd been so unhappy. Wow... had I been? If this evening was the bar, hell yes. I'd been miserable.

Not tonight, though. Tonight, I would savor her company. Raising my glass over my demolished slice of tiramisu, I cleared my throat to tear her away from her delicious treat. "All right, Geneva. Here's to working on brilliant ideas with one remarkable woman."

Chewing the last bite of her food, she dabbed at the upturned corners of her mouth. Her eyes were full of happiness, sparkling in the light from the flickering votives on the table.

"Here's to new friends." I loved watching her labor over words as she spoke, the Cupid's bow of her top lip serving as an anchor in their fullness. She clinked the edge of her second glass of wine to mine before we both took a drink.

"So, tell me something you haven't shared with me before," I asked, even though I didn't deserve to know. I was a shit in every sense of the word for not telling her the truth about who I was. But then it would all end.

"Hmm... I'm the oldest daughter. Um, my favorite color is emerald green. And my father and mother died due to his addictions. And no, this isn't *Two Truths and a Lie*."

The seemingly light question took a turn into something a little more introspective and darker than I'd expected, making me feel just a bit worse. No, I wouldn't be trying to sleep with her after such an intimate part of her life was revealed, thank you very much. "I don't know what... I'm sorry."

"Yeah, well... no, don't be. It's not something I share with people, because no one knows how to treat non-chemical addictions. You know? Like, oh, it would make more sense for him to be an alcoholic since he was speeding and driving recklessly. Somehow, running from a bookie due to thousands in debt is confusing... I don't know. Anyway... I'm not sure why I shared that with you. And now you have the pity look. I'm sorry. I shouldn't have told you. Those two glasses of wine are my limit because I tend to peel myself back like a can of sardines. Trust me, not many people like sardines."

I tried to give her an understanding smile and extended my hand across the table to gently wrestle the fork from her hands and web our fingers together. "It's okay. And I promise, I don't mind sardines one bit. In fact, they will be my preferred apocalypse food when the zombies come."

Despite her wet eyes, she grinned, then used a napkin to catch the tears yet to fall. "Oh Lord, I don't know how you do that. You make me smile even when I'm trying to be seriously distraught. It's a truly magical gift you have there, Mac."

Oh yeah... that was it. If I could just make her laugh once a day for the rest of my life, I would. In a New York minute. By the time the musicians took to the small stage after intermission, she'd somehow gotten another drink in her hand. *Oh boy.* That was something I should have watched for, especially when she started to dance.

# CHAPTER 12

## CALEB GREENE

*T*here were definitely better ways to end a date. I couldn't complain, though, since she was in my arms, just not in the way I'd wanted. I guided her down the walkway, the gentle summer breeze blowing against us. Our promenade should have been romantic, but I was as tight as a drum. Every part of me awakened with her pressed against me.

I needed to stop this, because she was too tipsy for anything, like at all, to happen between us. And for the love of God, did she have to smell so good?

"So, obviously, you aren't going to be taking the subway... let's get you into an Uber. Sound good?"

Geneva pulled away, looked up at me, and giggled. "Do you know who you look like?"

Her laugh made my heart race a bit, but I smothered the preemptive feeling of rejection and played along. "Nope. Who?"

"You look like that guy who plays the football player on that show I like." She smiled and allowed her gaze a leisurely drift down my body.

"Oh... that narrows it down." I fought the hell out of my grin, but I knew it still peeked through. "You have the Uber app on your phone?"

"I do... One sec." Her keys fell from her purse as she fished around for her cell. I leaned over to grab them, bumping my head on her purse as I came back up.

"Okay, workman's comp is in order." I laughed.

"Don't be silly." She poked at my chest with her finger. "We're not in the office. And I can't be held responsible for your off-hours injuries. However... I did find my cell." She handed it to me.

I took the handset and, with the other hand, took her arm to guide her again. I found the location, ordered the ride, then... "Um, you don't have an updated credit card on here..."

"I do too," she said, allowing her body to press against mine.

Lord, I should have gotten a medal for not kissing this woman. She was staring up at me as we walked, her eyes lit from within and a gentle smile on her full lips. It felt like we were on a date, and I allowed myself to indulge... to a point. "All right, let's check and see if it's the same. Where's your credit card?" She was silent for a moment, probably for a bit too long. I glanced down at her and saw her eyes had closed, just that quick.

"Geneva," I said, jostling her.

"Hmm," she moaned.

Oh, Jesus. The sound was heavenly, but this wasn't a good sitch. If I wasn't careful, I would compromise her. I could tell she was the type of person who liked her line in the sand to stay in place until she was ready. I looked around us and found a nearby bench. That way, we could find her credit card and I wouldn't have to risk her falling.

"Let's go over here for a moment." I guided her along and helped her sit. When I took a seat beside her, she immediately leaned her head on my shoulder. "That's better. Let's get you set up, shall we?"

Her response was a light snoring.

This was not what I'd planned. And even worse, I had a feeling she would begrudge the position she was in with me. The question was, did I rifle through her things looking for a credit card? Maybe I could just add one of mine. Nope, idiot. I would have to put my name in the app. I nudged her again. "Geneva, we've got to get you home."

"Okay, babe," she mumbled, then snuggled closer to me.

Several attempts later, it was clear this was not going to be easy. I'd run out of options. *Welp, Mac, this is another fine mess you've gotten us into...*

By the time we made it back to my fake place, she was resting as comfortably as one could in the back of a car positively reeking of cherry air freshener. Made a person wonder what scents lurked beneath the artificial sweetness. I cast aside my shudder at the thought and helped Geneva into my loft.

There were a million things running through my mind. Had I hidden all identifying documentation showing who I actually was? Were the sheets clean on the sofa bed? Did I feel like a world-class asshat for what I was doing?

After getting her settled and briefly wondering whether the mattress would be comfortable enough for her, I swept the room. The answer to all those questions from before was a resounding yes. Especially that last one.

I was a terrible dick for doing this. Part of me wanted to call the whole thing off. I'd taken a seat on the chair and begun pondering how I could easily exit without causing everyone I'd involved additional pain when a thing happened that shuttered the idea altogether.

Geneva stood and started to strip her clothes. "It's so warm in here..." She began to unbutton her top and reveal the silkiest brown skin in creation.

Two factions warred inside of me—one urged me to keep watching and the other reminded me that I was already an asshole and not to become a perv too. "I can turn the air conditioner up, I think..." I quickly got up to look for the thermostat, the one thing I hadn't checked since I'd arrived. I was from the Bay Area, after all, and I was never truly hot. Oh my God, she was, though. The jaunt around the room to find it gave me a chance to avert my eyes.

Peeking over my shoulder, I saw she was a) still standing, and b) given the view of her naked shoulder, completely undressed. I decided to fiddle with the thing until she was on the bed and hopefully, prayerfully, covered.

The loud springs let me know it was happening, so I turned. And good Lord, she had only covered her midsection—her breasts and her honey pot.

Okay, at least there was that.

I turned and walked over to her, trying so desperately to ignore the miles and miles of legs. She must have been created by an artist... She'd taken down her hair, and curls splayed from one end of the pillow to the other. Her eyes were closed, mouth slightly open, and I knew I could wake up to her looking just like that forever.

I fought over the lecherous beast who wanted to have her and spread the cover over the rest of her. She let out a satisfied murmur and I sent up a prayer of relief when the AC kicked on. It was already hot enough in there.

*Heavenly Father, give me the strength...*

# CHAPTER 13

## GENEVA CHAPMAN

*O*h, my God. My head felt like it had been shattered to pieces by a sledgehammer—though the hammer had apparently left my eyes intact enough for me to see that I was lying down on a strange bed. My stomach roiled at the thought of getting up to check out my surroundings. Even worse, I had no recollection of how I'd gotten stripped down to my undies. There was no light streaming in, so I assumed it wasn't fully dawn yet. That was unless I'd slept the sleep of the dead or slipped into a dimensional vortex and awakened a hundred light years later. Hadn't this been how Black Mamba woke up in *Kill Bill*? *"Wiggle your goddamn toe..."*

After another few moments, I found the strength to sit up on the ... pullout sofa? What happened? And where exactly was I?

Shit... I'd drunk too much the night before. In a flash, I knew what'd happened. I had had the third glass of wine. Son of a bitch. So, had I... Did I sleep with Mac? Oh no... no, no, no. I couldn't have. I would know, right?

Well, fuck. It had been so long since I'd hooked up with anyone, would I even remember?

*Yes, girl... you would fucking remember. Shit, you curse a lot when you're hungover... Okay, first... find a lamp so you can figure out where you are...*

Complying with my bossy internal thoughts, I found a lamp on a small table next to the couch. The room lit with a warm yellow glow once I flicked the switch. I looked around as far as the illumination reached. There was a coffee table, a huge desk, and glass block windows around the space. A makeshift closet was in the corner filled with button-down shirts neatly organized by color.

*Really? Who the hell organizes their closet by color?* And those were men's shirts... but I was in bed alone...

With a start, I sat upright, searching the room for what I feared. In a chair directly across from me was a body, the long figure sprawled uncomfortably sideways, legs draped over the side. I squinted against the residual headache aura and made out it was Mac. He was wrapped in what looked like a fleece throw, probably because the AC in his loft was set to *snow*.

Fuck me. I covered my mouth with a pillow from the pullout, smothering my initial panicked scream. *Fuck this. Fuck* wine. I pulled the blanket around myself and took a quick inventory of my body once more now that I was more awake. I mean, I trusted Mac. He had a kind way about him. He was helpful and solid, all the things I would want in a man... an intern, rather. I *didn't* trust myself around the guy sober. And when one wakes in a stupor, one must wonder if they had indeed behaved like a sexually liberated woman who'd drunk too damn much. Alas, nope. My WAP was safe, and still a WAP, since Mac looked simply enticing as he slept. The circumstances were infuriating... But was I mad because I'd allowed myself to be in a compromising situation with an employee, or because my WAP was intact?

First things first. I found the neat, folded pile of my clothes, then my bag on the desk, and I pulled out the toothbrush I carried with me for occasions when I awakened with a handsome man. I closed myself in the bathroom on the other side of a glass wall and brushed the yuck from last night away. I then slipped my clothes on and fluffed my hair. Two makeup wipes got rid of the ruined mascara and eyeliner. I glanced around the bathroom and noted the neatness of it. Since you never knew about the state of a man's apartment, I was impressed with his domestic skills. Before heading out, I applied a thin layer of lip gloss.

By the time I came out, Mac was awake and sitting upright in the chair. "Good morning," he said. His voice was gruff, and I noted a hint of morning sexy. He was rubbing his neck, probably smoothing out a kink given the state I'd found him in earlier.

"Morning..." I set my bag down on the desk and took a seat on the bed. I wanted to face him, because my God, who wouldn't? "I'm so sorry for making you responsible for me." Turns out, my shame only added to the pain in my head.

"No problem. I would have sent you home in a car, but you weren't in any state to ride off with some stranger. And I honestly couldn't find your wallet. Well, neither could you. So, I brought you back here. I hope you don't mind. And I did look away as you stripped out of your clothes. I am a gentleman, after all."

Relief washed over me. I didn't want him seeing me in the grandma-style, slimming panties I'd worn. "I appreciate all your help, and the fact that you're a gentleman. You don't meet many of your kind anymore." I waggled a finger in his direction.

"Oh yeah." Mac ran a hand over his head. "My mother wouldn't have it any other way. You know, she would have been seventy this year."

"She was old-school, huh?"

"Oh yeah, and she was not for the games. If she caught me being in any way disrespectful, she had a wooden cooking spoon with my name on it. She passed away from the flu a few years back." I could see unresolved mourning in his eyes.

"I'm so sorry. I know the pain of losing a parent." I fought against the urge to replay the events of my parents' death in my mind. I'd long since given up on forgetting the pain, but at least I had a bit more control over when I grieved.

"Yeah, it's honestly the worst thing to happen in the world. But at least she's at peace now. I still wonder though if there was something I could have done."

I wanted to hug him, but I was already sitting in his apartment with a hangover. I hated when people did all the obligatory things upon hearing of the loss of a parent. "Survivors' remorse. My counseling sessions gave me a name for it."

"I never went. Guess it didn't feel as if I had time. Then again, perhaps it was my incessant need to micro-manage everyone's shit." Truer words, apparently, because both of us laughed. In response, my traitorous body worked against me. Despite him not brushing his teeth, I wanted every part of him on my body.

"Trust me, I get the whole no-time thing. My sister tells me every chance she gets to live a little bit. There's just me and her, so she takes liberties with her advice." Discomfort with being so open with him cloaked me like a wet blanket. If I were operating on all cylinders, I probably would have been more focused on getting the ever-loving fuck out of his apartment. There was legit no way I would be able to explain this away if anyone found out. And Cliff would... oh my God, he would probably have my head.

"I get that." He looked down at the ever-present cell phone in his hand. "It's almost six. You might be early enough to avoid the walk of shame. Not that I want you to go."

I checked my own watch and found he was right. I needed to get home and change, and he was not making the situation any better. Inside, a battle was raging between my two sides—one part of me wanted to stay with him in his quaint little loft forever, having dinner then taking long walks in the park, but the other side, the smarter, responsible, intelligent part of me, knew none of that made any sense whatsoever. There was no way I'd done the right things last night, and it made no sense to double down the following morning.

"Yeah, I think you're right... thank you, though, for taking care of me last night. I am honestly embarrassed."

"No need to be embarrassed, and anytime, boss lady."

On that note, I got my ass out of there before I did something else to regret. Before I left, I gave him a smile and felt him behind me as he walked me out. I hadn't been conscious upon arrival and had time to see where he was living. I could tell the warehouse would soon be apartments, from the doorless units all along the hallway. The plumbing was being installed, and in another year or two, they would be worth millions of dollars in revenue.

At the end of the hall, his strong arm came around me and pressed the call button, and we waited. We were on the top floor, and I wondered exactly how many floors up we were. Back in his living space, I could easily see the Hudson, so we had to be pretty high up based on where he'd told me he lived.

Neither of us said a word, but for my part, there were so many things running through my mind. An image of him leaning in close and kissing me surfaced, and I didn't know whether it was a dream or reality. By the time I worked up the nerve to ask, the elevator was before me. I stepped on and so did he, then he pulled the gate down before the doors closed us in. I swallowed the desire to ask. Some things were, after all, better left unsaid.

## CHAPTER 14

### CALEB GREENE

*M*onday couldn't get there soon enough. I'd spent the weekend discussing strategy with Owenthal and thinking of Geneva. I wanted to do so many things with her, *to her*. It had been all I could do to resist her for the duration of her visit with me. She was epically fine as hell. Now, on the way to the office, I had her on my mind heavy. My dick was semi-hard, which would only get worse when I was around her. There was no way I was going to be able to leave her in a few weeks if I continued on this path. Even as I said the words, I knew I didn't want to. My life was a mess, though. I stood to lose everything I had, and then where would I be? I didn't even know who I wanted to be. Surely not in a place for a serious relationship. Who saw that coming? And why the fuck was I even speaking in terms of a relationship?

On Monday morning, I was supposed to meet up with Dex, so thankfully, I was able to get Sam to pick me up after a mad dash around the loft to get dressed. "Thanks, man," I yelled to Sam from the passenger door.

The driver tipped his hat and then turned around to get the car in gear once I closed the door. He really was a decent dude.

I headed inside, glad I'd decided to leave the house early and beat Geneva to work. I didn't want her walking up on Dex and me chatting it up. The explanation for being in Dex's stratosphere would be hard to come by. I rarely saw him during the workday. I didn't want too many people to pick up our friendly demeanor. It would make things difficult for Geneva.

I made it upstairs and found Dex seated behind his desk. He was almost as much of a workaholic as I was. "What's up, my guy?"

I pushed the door closed behind me, suddenly aware of Dex's office being a fishbowl. When I stepped inside, I fought against the urge to adjust the temperature. Had to be seventy-five degrees in there. Naturally, he had a manual setting separate from the rest of the building, and when I saw the person beside him, I understood the reason for the extra heat in the room.

"Hi there, sweetheart." I walked over to her and rustled her hair, waiting for the wide eyes to stare up at me. Georgina looked just like her mother in that instant. Other times, she was the spitting image of Dex. Regardless of who she looked like at the moment, she was adorable.

"Hi, Unkal Cwaleb."

I couldn't help the laugh at her efforts. She was positively cherubic. She raised her chubby arms up to wrap around me, and I scooped her up, letting her get her fill of playing with my face, pulling my cheeks down, and touching the very tip of her finger to the tip of my nose.

"She likes me."

"Don't get excited. She thinks you're an Octonaut." Clearly, the man delighted in telling me this.

"What's an Octonaut?"

"Oh, it's a great show. You should come by and watch it for a few hours... or years."

"Thanks. I'll pass."

I sat on the floor with her in my arms next to a pile of every toy known to man and turned to face Dex, who was clearly wrapped around Georgina's finger from the way he was gushing. Couldn't blame him. "Isn't this early for her?"

"No, apparently. She seems to be a morning person and Mommy has a cold, so I just came in to grab some things. Enough about me. What warranted a call instead of a text to me yesterday? Sorry I couldn't talk, by the way." He leveled a glance loaded with suspicion at me before returning his attention to whatever was on the large, curved screen of his desktop.

"Nothing. Just needed to think some things through. Wanted to get your thoughts."

"Yup, you have like eighty-five percent of my attention."

"Thinking about this lawsuit..." I walked over to the chair and practically fell into it. "I don't know where to go with it. Part of me feels like I shouldn't be fighting him on it, and the other part feels like he has some goddamn nerve."

"Gonna keep it real with you. I honestly thought it was about that girl."

Better to play dumb on that one. "That girl?"

"Yeah... you know... the one who has a millionaire masquerading around like a college student. Never mind your age. You don't even have the capacity to appear broke. It's not in you. And, might I add, she *is* so going to find out."

"Shees gowing toho find owt." The little princess clearly agreed with her father. I glanced down at her and found her making her stuffed animal fly through the air.

Dex let out a chuckle, enjoying his echo in the mini-him.

"Thankfully, that's not what the conversation is about." I sat forward in the chair and ran my hands over my hair.

"Avoidance only gets you so far. But you're right. We're talking about handing over part of your wealth. And I can't tell you what to do about it. I can tell you that if this is ego, you should seriously consider how far you're willing to take it. You know? It's been a long time since he was your partner. It could be that he's just out of money. If you're not over him walking out the way he did, try to evaluate if that wasn't the best thing for the sake of the company."

"He knew my mom had just died and waited until I was away dealing with that to undermine me. He sold our programming and gave Optisoft an advantage in the market. I'm still working out the mess he created."

"He made a bad decision, yes. But if it weren't for him, consider where you would be. And as I recall, Optisoft couldn't even win with the additional leverage they bought. Aren't they out of business?"

"Yeah. Like a year after it all went down. And now that son of a"—I glanced down at the princess before proceeding—"bucket has the nerve to come back and demand half?"

"It's the nature of the beast. He's obviously struggling. And that makes a difference in the size of your balls."

"Yeah, he got a pair made of titanium."

"Where's the balls, Daddy?" The tiny voice reminded us both of our language.

"No, honey." Dex leaned down and got eyeball to eyeball with his mini. "We left them home. I promise we'll head there in a minute. Okay, buddy?"

"'Kay, Daddy."

"Well, I'll let you finish here. I think we've colored her vocabulary enough. Besides, I need to get downstairs before boss lady gets in. Can't have her thinking I'm schmoozing up here."

"Good idea. There's no favoritism at Montague. And did you just call her *boss lady*?"

"Never. I'll catch you later."

"Have a good day at school, champ."

I didn't bother to flip him off. With my luck, his little girl would repeat the gesture, and I didn't need that kind of static with Bianca. Anyway, it was almost eight thirty. For safe measure, I went all the way down then rode back up so if anyone was just off the elevator, they would see an up arrow and not a down. I didn't want any of them to think I had an unfair advantage.

I made it to my desk undetected, and there she was. She didn't look disheveled at all despite what had gone down between us. Maybe she wasn't as bothered as I was. I'd hardly slept with her inches away from me. For all I knew, I was probably the only one slipping and falling into my feelings.

I couldn't resist the urge to go in and talk to her. Rapping a knuckle on the open glass door of her office, I called out, "Good morning."

"Morning," she said. A red tint started to glow in her cheeks.

A tide of mischief took over as I wondered exactly how deep that blush went and if it was visible all over, down to the lighter patch of skin on the back of her calf... "You look rested. What did you do last night?"

Her eyes widened, and I was right—she'd been thinking about our night together too. I watched her, the desire to ruin her lipstick strong, her mouth beckoning. "Nothing. I um... just played video games with my sister."

"Yeah. Video games can be all-consuming," I said.

Geneva gave me a light smile and returned her attention to her computer. I couldn't blame her, since even I knew I was acting a bit weird. Better get to the point, since I was losing her attention fast, and wasn't she the whole reason I was there in the first place? "I wanted to know... You said you like pop music, and since we did the whole jazz thing, I was thinking it would be fair to ask if you wanted to head over to Jersey to see BTG? They're playing there tonight, and my buddy sets up concerts... he hooked me up with front-row seats." I watched her reaction go from excited to confused, then back to neutral.

"I um... I don't know if that's a good idea. I mean, people could misconstrue our relationship if they were to ever find out... It's not that I don't want to go. It's just the optics."

I could have kicked myself. I should have foreseen someone like her being concerned with compromising all her hard work for some intern. Even worse, I would have to tell Dex he was absolutely right. I shouldn't have put myself in this position, let alone putting Montague at risk. "Oh, yeah. Well, I agree. It could be misconstrued. I would never want to put your position in jeopardy." I waited for her to give me some sign she liked me. Part of me was ready to give up this charade, but even thinking it gave me chest pains.

"So." She squirmed in her chair and shifted to face her computer. "I have a planning session today. You are welcome to join in. No man is an island, so working on teams will be a valuable experience."

"Oh, um..." The thought of sitting across the table from people who didn't work for me was hard-line. I didn't have it in me not to lead. "I think I'll take a pass on this one. I have some work to do—"

"Oh no, Mac. That's not a question. It's an assignment." She wasn't looking at me when she said it, her face lit from the screen and her body tense. Was it possible I'd pushed her too far? I was pretending, after all. For her, this was her job. Professionalism had to be maintained.

"Yeah, okay. I'll be there. Could you forward the invite? I'll just be outside at my desk if you need me." With that, I turned and walked out of her office, half expecting her to stop me.

Here's a clue—she didn't. That probably bothered me more than her demand. The thing was, it also turned me on.

# CHAPTER 15

## GENEVA CHAPMAN

*W*hen Mac left, my heart sank. Truth was, I was getting sloppy. I'd spent the entire weekend lamenting over slipping up with him. And wondering whether Cliff was right. I'd gotten too close and managed to let my guard down with an employee. What kind of example was I setting if I preyed on someone who had less power than I did? If I were a man and he were some innocent intern, I would be crucified. So, I needed to draw the line. I had been bound and determined to do so, if only to save him from a future of going into a professional place of work and preying on women who worked with him. I was supposed to be teaching him, not screwing him. But my abrupt change in demeanor probably was too harsh. Damn. Why was it so hard to strike a balance with him? Why did I care so much? Why hadn't I met him in some other setting? I would have gone with him to see BTG in a heartbeat. And not just because they were my favorite group.

Hopefully, he wasn't sulking... or hurt? I glanced around the side of my monitor to check on him and, thanks to the glass offices, I could easily see him typing away. I could also easily see his forearms, a light dusting of hair over them, his fingers moving over the keys... clicking the mouse. I was so very envious of his hardware.

Just when I was about to stop staring at him, he turned. And caught me. *Dammit...* My heart sank and I straightened in my chair, ensuring my face was safely hidden behind my oversized monitor. Lord, I was just hopeless. He probably thought I was someone who could benefit from some time on a therapist's couch. I mean, I was... but I could at least try to hide it better.

I was saved from my thoughts by a chime—a text notification. Maybe if I looked like I was texting someone, we could pretend like he didn't just catch me staring at him. I picked the phone up and found a message from Leddie. The visible subject line read "Don't get in trouble messing with the intern..." She must have been some kind of mind reader. I opened it to read the rest of the message.

**Leddie**: But that's not what I'm texting you for. I moved into the final round of AppTech's contest. Just got the email. *grabby hands emoji*

**Me**: For real? That is so AWESOME *party hat emoji* I'm so proud.

**Me**: P.S. I'm not messing with him. You'd be proud of me too. Very professional.

**Me**: *Female Judge emoji*

**Leddie**: Thank you. I can't believe it.

**Leddie**: Also, I don't believe you overlooked his thighs...

**Me:** That was me on the weekend. Monday morning Gigi is smarter. Focused.

**Leddie**: Okay, girl. I'm going to work on the bugs in the storyboard for FV. C u tonight.

**Me**: \*waving hand emoji\*

I put the phone down and forbade myself from sneaking a peek at Mac's thigh bulge. I was probably hopeless. I was like that Lizzo song. Like all of them. Instead of focusing on him, I dug into my work. I sent him the meeting invite from Outlook, then began comparing integration platforms for the security migration. I must say, I did a little better. I only thought of him another thirty or forty times before lunch. Sigh.

BEFORE I KNEW IT, IT WAS TIME FOR THE MEETING. IT should be a crime to have morning meetings on Mondays. At least it was the last thing standing between me and lunch. I desperately needed to get out and take a walk. Maybe I'd go visit Pepe's and get some deep-fried corn stuffed with cheese, sour cream, and green chili. Yes, for sure. I needed to drown myself in lots of calories. After all, when you're deprived of the thing you want, go to the thing you can get. Sure, I would pay later, but honestly, I needed to eat my lust.

"Want to walk over to the meeting with me?" Mac was standing in my office doorway.

A wave of heat rushed over my face. It was almost as if he knew when and what I was thinking of him. "What? Why?" *Yeah, because that's not defensive at all.*

"Oh... I mean, I don't know where the conference room is, if I'm being honest." His brows furrowed as he looked at me.

"Yup, it's in the main conference room. We can head over together. I'd just assumed you'd had your orientation in there too." I focused on keeping my voice smooth and even. He didn't need to know he affected me every time he walked into the room. I was a boss. I was a leader. Completely in control.

"No, I went to HR."

Yup, that's the foolish look. I knew I had it just from the way he was staring at me. Sheesh, I needed to be professional. Not a total bitch. "Sure. Let me just um..." I gathered up my work badge and my padfolio and stood, smoothing my pencil skirt, which was probably hella wrinkled since I hadn't moved all morning. Not even for my beloved coffee. I couldn't bear to walk past him. "Okay. All set."

Mac didn't say anything, just extended his arm out in an "after you" motion. I obliged and felt the weight of his stare as I passed him in the doorway and moved down the hallway. We were going to be terrible in there together. It was a shitty idea to invite him, but I mostly wanted to show Cliff I wasn't being jaded. Mac was a hard worker and only needed to be fairly judged. I wasn't so hot for him that I couldn't make good decisions. Was I?

CALEB GREENE

Obviously, I was losing ground with her. I was shook by the change in her, but... okay, I had to understand it. Maybe it was due to the drinking. Honestly, if I were to go back in time, I wouldn't change a thing. I enjoyed my time with her. I should have been ashamed of my actions since I'd been essentially lying the whole time I'd known her, and honorable Mac cared, but Caleb, my true heart and soul, was greedy as hell. He wasn't going to let go.

The truth was, I liked Geneva so much. I didn't care about other people's opinions of me and her. We were being appropriate. I couldn't help that our chemistry was in tune with one another. I reacted to her, and I knew she reacted to me. And while I felt it, I wasn't in the business of forcing women to be with me. As much as I wanted something to happen between the two of us, it couldn't only be me. Maybe my fake internship was a way to insulate myself? If she were to reject me, I could go on about my business, no harm, no foul. Couldn't I?

We arrived at the conference room and I sat on one of the seats along the wall instead of at the huge boardroom table. I wanted to be there but not. To blend in. That was the important thing.

Cliff came in and blanched. He took one look at me, and all the color drained from his face. He walked stiffly to his seat, gripping the tablet he carried under his arm with his free hand, then flinging it onto the table. I wanted to remind him the screen was glass, but I was also trying not to ruffle any feathers.

I didn't need that in my life.

"Morning, all," Cliff said. He glanced around at the eight or so men seated at the table. They were all carbon copies of each other—wearing the same dark blue or black tailored suits, their hair cut longer on top, shorter on the sides, and their eyes disinterested. "I see we have a visitor today," Cliff continued, nodding his head in my direction. The rest of the room glanced at me, and I gave a stiff nod back.

"Mac is an intern on Geneva's team and here with us. I realize some of you have yet to meet him. Please, take a few moments to introduce yourself."

I knew Cliff wasn't trying to be a dickhole, but a flash of panic sent heat rushing over my neck. None of them spared me too long of a glance. Most of them had already returned their attention to Cliff. I was glad too, because I worried whether any of them would recognize me. I had done a pretty good job of maintaining my identity, concealing myself from the world, so far. When they didn't give me a second look, a little of my tension abated. "I'm Macaulay Berger. Please call me Mac. I'm an intern and—"

Cliff let out a snort, which he seemed to cover by coughing. It interrupted my flow. Couldn't really blame him then, either. After all, he knew my dirty secret and I'd lifted that name from a fast-food bag. I honestly deserved what I got from him. Before I could continue, though, I heard Geneva clear her throat.

"Yes, he is actually an incredible team member. He is ingenious at identifying process solutions. I'm very pleased to have him on my team." When Geneva spoke, her colleagues' faces loosened. Obviously, they trusted her, even if she hadn't been there for a long while. And I was thankful to her for stepping to the plate when I had no voice. Not many people would have done that. Naturally, I would have recovered, but I'd never had a pinch hitter before, and it was... breathtaking.

For the rest of the meeting, I struggled not to betray my years of experience in the IT industry. I added in a few suggestions, not wanting to make Geneva regret her words, but nothing to make myself look like a wiseass either.

By the end, I could feel her become a little warmer with me. As we broke away from the pack, I slowed my pace to walk beside her back to her office. "Um... thanks for what you did in there."

She looked up at me but didn't break her stride. "He was being a jerk to you. As a member of my team, I can't let that happen." Her lips curved on the ends, almost as if she'd enjoyed sticking it to Cliff. It was a mild skewering, but a skewering, nonetheless.

"Well, while I appreciate it, I don't want you defending me. You just started here. I'll be gone and you'll still have to deal."

"That's the thing. I'll always have to deal. I may as well ensure the people who report to me are protected. That's what being a leader is, Mac."

"Okay, well... may I offer to buy lunch in return for your chivalry?"

"Maybe," she said, heading into her office. "What did you have in mind?"

As she walked, it was as if I were tethered to her. I was trapped in her orbit, her the sun, and I was... some tiny little star. And it was cool for me. I'd never been one to gravitate to a person—so far in my life, I'd been the one leading. But I would... follow her anywhere. My phone chimed, and I pulled it out to see who was texting. It was Owenthal.

"You pick," I said, staring at my cell. The mediator was ready to meet with us after reviewing the deposition. I tapped in a speedy reply telling him to set the date... quickly.

"Did you need to take that?" I glanced up at her then. She was seated behind her desk, the sun streaming in on her face, almost as if she were an angel.

"No, I can get it later. I have an appointment to follow up on, no biggie." Lame, I know. But it was the only thing I could think of. I honestly couldn't take feeding her another line.

"I see. Well, we can go back to the food trucks. There's another I wouldn't mind trying."

I made a face before I could catch myself.

"Don't grimace. You know you loved it last time. You out-of-towners will get enough of looking down your nose at our street food. It's the best in the world. I'm sure of it."

"I think Greece would disagree with you there." Goddamn, sometimes I could kick my own ass.

"I'm sure Greece has its finer points, but we aren't to be messed with, I can assure you. When did you go to Greece?"

Fuck. I was going to get caught being so free with her. I absolutely wanted to share everything with her. "Spring break." Which technically wasn't a lie because I had been there once on spring break.

"Well, in that case, let's go have Greek food. I've never been to Greece, but I do know a good place. You've put me in the mood for it."

"Can't say no to that. I'll go and respond to a few emails on the integration and be ready whenever you are."

"Great. Just need about a half hour."

"Cool." Like an idiot, I rapped on the door twice and turned away. As if she didn't already know I was stoked just being with her. What a douche canoe.

"Oh, and Mac..."

I nearly tripped turning back around to face her. "Yup..."

"Unfortunately, this can only be as friends. You do

know that, don't you? I mean, just because the concert was more expensive doesn't change the optics."

Something about that comment set my chest ablaze. "Oh... I mean, yeah. Of course," I said, my hand instinctively rubbing the invisible slice her knife-sharp words had left.

# CHAPTER 16

## GENEVA CHAPMAN

*W*hat the hell was wrong with me? I knew good and well I wasn't supposed to go out to lunch with Mac. He was an *intern*. And it was lame. So lame to go to lunch with someone who I'd just lectured about optics a few hours before. At least lunch could be explained away. But could it, though?

"How's your lamb?" Mac had been staring at his phone for the majority of the meal, which wasn't like him. He was normally so... attentive. But was it right of me to pry when I'd been busy all day trying to put some distance between us?

"Oh, no... it's good." He finally placed his phone face-down on the white tablecloth. "I was unloading the BTG tickets." He shifted his eyes when he said it, so I knew, without a doubt, I'd upset him.

"I'm sorry again about that. You know about conflict of interest, right? Say, if I were to recommend you stay on with Montague, HR would look at me accepting the tickets as some kind of quid pro quo. It just leaves us vulnerable... It leaves *you* vulnerable too. I hope you understand." That was fair enough, wasn't it? I left out that setting boundaries was for my own safety, to protect me from potentially slipping into some feelings for him.

"It's cool. Really. I shouldn't have put you in that position, and I do know a little about ethics violations. No need to apologize. You're smart to turn me down. Now, there's a string of words I never thought I'd say." And somehow, Mac had me giggling just seconds after I heard his contagious laughter.

"Great. I'm so glad. You're too nice of a person, and hurting you would be the last thing I would want."

"Well, cheer up a bit because I'm not that nice. Just ask anyone who really knows me." His eyes shifted down to his plate for a few moments before he picked up his knife and fork again.

"Now, why am I struggling to believe you?" This time, when I laughed, he didn't.

Mac kept right on cutting up his lamb chops.

To be honest, the silence was uncomfortable, even for me. While I shouldn't have been prying, I couldn't help myself. "So, did you unload the tickets, or are you stuck with them?"

"I got rid of them. Turns out, they are pretty popular. My buddy is taking his wife."

"Oh wow, they're married straight out of college?"

"Huh? Oh... well, um, sometimes you just meet someone, and you know they're the one for you."

"Now that is heartening. I can't say I've had that experience." I pushed my rice around on my plate a bit. It was my turn to clam up. I wasn't about to leave my petticoat out for him to see again.

"I think... I mean, I used to be skeptical about relationships too. I would say there was always time for one.

Always next year or when the moment was right. But I realized—recently, I believe—that when you want something, it doesn't make sense to wait for all the cards to fall into place. You should act on it. World be damned." He swallowed hard after he spoke; his eyes damn near pleaded. It was as if every word were somehow vital to him... and to me.

I let out a hard laugh, discomfort getting the better of me. "Wow. World be damned, huh? See, I wish I could do that. I'm way more guarded than that."

"More leftovers from your mom and dad's relationship?"

"Maybe. I'm a skeptic like you were, I guess. Perhaps I'll graduate to your level of enlightenment one day," I said, squirming a bit in my seat.

"Here's to enlightenment," he said, holding his water up in my direction.

"Cheers." As the lips of the glasses touched, I, despite myself, hoped he was right.

We managed to finish our lunch within the hour, unlike when we'd gone to the park. We were making good time walking at a fast clip back to the office when I heard a sound. I grabbed Mac's arm and pulled him to the side so the other pedestrians could pass. Nothing was worse than stopping in the middle of a throng of people in Manhattan.

He obliged me, staring at me hard, probably in an effort to figure out what was going on.

"Shhh," I said. "Just listen..." A faint cry cut through the sounds. "Did you hear that?"

It was his turn to strain against the noise from all the foot and vehicular traffic. I heard a whimpering, not human but... I stepped out onto the sidewalk. There, at the end of the alley, was a rustling. "Found it." I took off down the alley, despite the robust scents.

"Wait up, Geneva." I heard both Mac's voice and his heavy footsteps as he scrambled behind me.

I had to keep going, though. Those were sounds of distress, not something normal. When I reached the middle of the alley, I saw what was making the noise. And, oh my God. A small pack of black fur stuck out beneath a plastic garbage bag. Poor thing must have been sleeping there in the alley or had gotten trapped beneath one of the restaurant trash bags trying to get food. The cat let out another meow that was guttural and soul-shattering, as if it knew we'd come on a search-and-rescue mission.

"Help me get it out, Mac," I said, scrambling through the debris and smelly bags. Nothing says New York like eighty-degree days pre-garbage pick-up.

"Don't climb up there. Let me do it." He grabbed my arm when I was mid-climb and helped me back down to the ground. "Montague can replace me, but they need you."

I was too worried about the cat to dispute his self-deprecating comment. "Well, you be careful too."

After moving more of the debris, I saw him bend at the waist and pull up a... a tiny little kitten. He could hold him in two hands. Mac handed him down to me, and I instantly started picking the lettuce and dirt bits out of his fur. He was all black with a small white patch on his chest. The poor thing was panting and practically skin and bones. "Oh my God, he's in pretty bad shape. We need to feed him."

Mac jumped down—with fantastic agility, might I add—from the piles of garbage. "You think he's all right for us to be handling? He could be... you know, covered with fleas."

I picked through his fur, looking for bugs and ticks. "No, he doesn't seem to be, but just in case, we can give him a bath. We'll have to smuggle him back into the office."

"Smuggle him in? What if people have cat allergies, or there's something wrong with him?" His face was screwed up, disdain as evident as the stink in the alleyway.

Damned if I wanted to admit it, but he was right. I couldn't compromise others in the workplace. It would have been irresponsible. "So... you take him to your place. I'll tell them you had an emergency if anyone asks. You could take him to your place maybe and then... clean him up and feed him? I can bring some things when I'm off?" It was a huge imposition, but I couldn't fathom leaving a poor defenseless kitten out in the cold. Okay, granted it was summer, but he'd almost been murdered by garbage bags. "We need to save him."

Mac didn't look as convinced. He was wiping at his pants, which were covered with what looked like marinara sauce. At least, I hoped it was marinara sauce. "We should probably take him to the pound."

"No... I won't do that." The pound was a hard no for me. My chest tightened at the thought. I knew it was my childhood rearing its ugly head, but this was a kitten. I couldn't leave him. "Uh-uh. I am going to find a place for him, despite my sister's allergies, whether you help me or not. I feel like... it's the least I could do."

Mac immediately crossed his arms, glowering at both me and the cat. The cat, however, didn't seem to notice. He, or she, was nestling in against my bosom. I didn't know about Mac, but I was already a goner. "I don't know, I feel like that's risky. I'm pretty sure Cliff already hates me a little bit. I don't want to give him more of a reason."

"You don't have to worry about him. You report to me. And I'm giving you the time off. I just need some room to figure this out for... for Fluff."

"No, please don't name him. Once you name it, it's too late."

"Well, there you have it. You have to take Fluff to your place, and I will come over tonight and take care of him. By then, I'll have it all figured out."

"This is a bad idea," he said, shifting his weight in frustration, his arms still crossed over his chest.

"I think it's the only idea because I can't, in good conscience, leave this cat out here to be harmed or worse. He's so little and defenseless." I could feel the tears welling and there's not much that could still make me cry after losing both parents in a car crash and watching my sister struggle to put her life back together again. "And... you can't go into the office with whatever that is on your pants. Can you?" That last bit left me feeling a little satisfied with myself. "It's only for a night... two days, tops."

"Fine." Finally, he dropped his arms and held them out for Fluff.

I couldn't believe how adorable the kitty was. Before handing him over, I searched his hair for a collar. He didn't have one and looked to be only a few weeks old. Unless he was just that malnourished. Finding no identifying markers on his body, I handed him over to Mac. He looked like the thing was going to explode. "You look a little uncomfortable. Have you ever had a pet before?"

"No, never."

"Oh, that's too bad."

"I honestly don't like being responsible for other living things. I don't have a good track record. All my house plants have died, and when I had a goldfish, he met an untimely end due to a five-day marathon of *Call of Duty*. And they're not particularly neat."

"Mac, you live in a warehouse. Did you ever think of what's below you on those abandoned floors?"

"Nope. And to be honest, I keep my area clean and I'm hardly there. They can stay in their place, and I'll stay in mine. Bringing the cat in is probably asking for trouble." Almost as if on cue, Fluff started licking Mac's hand. It was like watching an iceberg spontaneously break apart.

"Fine, I'll take him. This means, however, that you'll have to hit my power button on my laptop and put it in my desk drawer. Compliance matters, after all. But, girl, we're going to find somewhere for him to be, because as cool as you are, and cute with your watery eyes, we cannot have a cat without some kind of lifelong commitment or something. Cats live like fifteen years." Mac's lips formed a tight line, but he was rubbing Fluff.

"Oh, yay. And listen, I feel you. I get where you're coming from. I will for sure get the cat out of your house," I said, knowing I would have to make good on my word just from the many facial tics developing on Mac's mug. "I promise I will make this up to you. Promise, promise, promise."

Mac released an audible sigh. "Yeah, yeah. Go ahead back to work so you can wash your hands. No sense in both of us getting the plague from all that garbage."

"I'll pray for your continued health, Typhoid Mary."

Oh, he didn't look happy at all. "Right."

"Okay, thanks again. I'll text you when I'm leaving.

I'll try not to be too long. Oh, and can you send me your address? I forgot to get it um... that other time."

"I don't think you were in any position to get it, so no worries. I'll send it in a sec. And... you're welcome." He rolled his eyes a bit, indicating his level of protest.

"All right, see you soon," I said. "And seriously, thank you, Mac."

I had to tear myself away from those two. I wanted nothing more than to stay with Mac and help him with Fluff. He was so cute. Oh... and Fluff too... I hurried away, putting more distance between me and just one more reason to *like* the hell out of Mac.

## CHAPTER 17

### CALEB GREENE

"Thanks again, man," I said to Sam, exiting the car. Once I'd called Dex, and he stopped laughing—he'd especially loved the part where Geneva called me Typhoid Mary—he loaned me the use of his driver and car so Fluff and I could get home without sitting in filth for too long. For fuck's sake, I hoped and prayed that was *actually* marinara sauce. Both me and the cat smelled like a sewer.

Sam simply gave me a smile and a wave as he quietly drove away... probably headed straight for a carwash. Damn, I was making an ass of myself for this woman when she was never going to involve herself with an intern. And apparently, from the way I was smiling at the cat, I enjoyed every minute of it.

Sad thing was, if I'd come clean in the beginning, I wouldn't be in the situation. And time was running short. Owenthal had texted that the mediation would take place early the following week. It was rapid, and while I thought I knew what I wanted, I was still a bit unsure.

Now, with the cat and things spiraling out of my

control, I needed to make some decisions. I should have just manned up to my fears over the case and told her who I was. Then there'd been the other fear... what if she only wanted me for what I have? So many women did that to me, I was gun shy AF. The veil of anonymity had just seemed safer at the time.

If I were being honest, I would have realized that I was obviously sorry for all the lies, all the games... Which would be the only reason I crawled around in a pile of trash and was taking home a furball. The pang in my chest echoed the truth of it. Geneva didn't deserve to be lied to, and I felt bad about it. New feeling for me, and if I were more enlightened, I probably would have written the shit in a journal somewhere and contemplated the implications of it all.

I looked down at the bundle of fur in my arms. Before we'd come home, Sam took me by Pet Stop, and I grabbed everything known to man to clean the kitty up, along with some playthings. And a ball. And a cat tower I'd have to put together. My hands were loaded, but I wasn't putting the cat down. If he ran, there's no telling what he could get into. Geneva had probably been right about the lower abandoned floors. I shuddered at the thought.

Fluff looked back up at me as if to ask what the hell I was waiting on?

"Fine. Let's go see your new digs. And no complaining, because I'm the one that has to live here. You're just visiting, with your lucky ass."

After some careful maneuvering, I had the cat and all his luxury items up the elevator to our spot. I closed the door and got him set up before feeding him. For such a small little thing, he ate like a linebacker. Caving, I gave him a little more in the bowl then poured him some vitamin-fortified, specially formulated cat milk. I hoped he didn't get used to that because six months of the stuff would cost as much as a Bentley.

Once we were all done modifying my faux abode into a cat palace, I gave him a bath in the shower stall. Fun fact —cats hate baths. After several scratches and a sprint around the tiny space, where I bumped my head no less than forty times, I finally got him to think it was his idea.

I dragged the nozzle down and sprayed it against the wall. Once he thought we were playing, he jumped into the water. Picking him up, I shampooed him and started the game again. An hour and a half later, he was cuddled in a brand-new blanket on top of a microfiber cat mattress that promised not to damage his fur.

Fluff was probably the best kept stray in Manhattan.

I, on the other hand, still looked a mess. Glancing down at my phone, I saw it was no less than one hour before Geneva got off work. Considering she was excited as all get-out and had promised to leave early, I needed to get myself successfully *defunked* and tetanus free.

I cleaned the bathroom and showered in under forty-five minutes, which must have been some kind of record, considering what Fluff had done to the place. Just as I leaned back on the couch to rest for a bit, a text notification went off.

I looked at my phone, and sure enough, it was Geneva. Fluff even raised his sleepy head for a few moments as if in anticipation. "Back off, cat. I met her first."

Fluff let out a low purr in response.

**Geneva:** Hey there. You guys okay? How's Fluff? <black cat emoji>

**Me:** Fine, fine. His scratches hurt like a SOB tho.

**Geneva:** Oh no. <afraid emoji> What'd you do to him to make him scratch you?

**Me:** Not a damn thing. I told you he was feral.

**Geneva:** SMH. Okay, send me your address. I figured you were busy.

**Me:** <drops location pin>

**Me:** That's easier.

**Geneva:** Okay. Thx. See u in a min.

I contemplated for more than a few moments on messaging her back and saying... something. I mean, I was nervous for her. I knew she didn't want to risk her job, so I would have to figure out a way to let it go. To let *her* go. Given Geneva's views on liars, there was no way out. How would I bow out gracefully when it was all said and done? It would be best if she didn't have to find that out about me, but if the case went badly, or worse, I was publicly outed, I would be no better with her anyway. The superior choice was to end my suffering sooner rather than ripping the bandage off over time. Dropping my phone, I leaned back on the couch.

Since the mediation was only a few days from now, I resolved to enjoy what little time I had left with Geneva. Even if she was the most effervescent woman I'd ever met. She set my soul on fire... There was so much more I wanted to know about her. I was changing and doing new things. Like... not having Cliff drawn and quartered and taking the subway. I liked seeing her smile. As pissed as I was over dumpster diving, it was wonderful to see her smiling. I was still getting rid of Fluff, though. Oh, Geneva...

Warmth right in the center of my chest, along with a tiny set of claws, pulled me from my thoughts. I looked down, careful not to freak Fluff out, and found him making himself at home on my stomach. "Hundred-dollar mattress not good enough for you, huh?"

He only meowed in response. Despite myself, I put a hand on his head and stroked the fur along his spine. His purring sounded like a tiny little engine running.

Well, dammit. I couldn't let the cat wrap me around his paw too. I should have put him back in his bed, but he looked so... comfortable. Instead, the both of us sat there waiting for our favorite person to arrive.

About a half hour later, to my surprise, my text notification fired off and it was Geneva. Fluff and I went to the door to retrieve her. Shit, she must have run all the way here.

"Hey... how'd you get here so fast?"

"Oh, I um, took a cab."

"But you hate cabs."

"Yeah, but I adore Fluff." Geneva extended her hands, and Fluff practically leapt into her arms. No shit, he didn't even wait for me to let him go.

"Traitor..." I rolled my eyes and led both of them down the hallway.

All the way up, they cooed and cuddled with one another until we got into my space. "Oh my God, did you buy everything?"

"Well... I figured he wouldn't get into trouble if he had a lot to do. And I made him an appointment for his shots this weekend at Pet Stop." My discomfort had me rubbing a hand over my head and looking away from her suspicious stare.

"I thought you didn't like kitties."

"Oh, I don't. He couldn't very well be relocated somewhere without everything he needs, right?"

"Um-hmm. Fluff, I think you have a reluctant fan. And how could you not, you little cutie?" she said, holding him up into the air with both hands.

All I could think of in that moment was the circle of life. "Yeah, well, I fed him. As you can probably smell, bathed him too. And I'm pretty sure that wasn't marinara sauce."

"Oh, I'm so sorry. I'll pay your dry-cleaning bill."

"Don't worry. I cut those clothes off me and tossed them into the incinerator to make sure they didn't come back to life."

"Tune in next week to *The Walking Twill*." She laughed, holding the cat up to her face and giving him a kiss. Pretty sure Fluff, the little shit, was giggling too based on the look on his face.

"Anyway, you want some water or something? I've got flat and sparkling..."

"That's just so interesting. I don't think I know of a single graduate student who calls it flat water. Were you a waiter before?"

Dammit. "Yup. Even with a scholarship, sometimes you need help making ends meet."

"Figured. Yeah, I had some doozies myself while working through school and taking care of myself and Leddie. Some of them were completely awful. Like the one selling knives door to door, which I hated because I didn't like talking people into buying stuff they couldn't afford. I tried to stick to richer neighborhoods. In all fairness, though, those were incredible knives. I still have one of the demos, and it can cut through the bone of a steak."

"Impressive." I didn't know what else to say. Somehow, every lie I told Geneva hurt a bit more. "Well, at least we know who Fluff's favorite is," I said, shifting the subject.

"Oh, I'm sure I'm not his favorite."

"Tell me something. Do you know whether it's a boy or not?"

"Um... no. He just feels like a boy," she said. Geneva turned around and headed to the couch. She kicked her heels off and slid her skirt up a bit before flopping down and sitting on her feet with Fluff on her lap.

"All right, but I'm just saying. He fights like a girl."

"And how would you know how girls fight?"

"I've watched women's professional boxing, and it's way more vicious than men's boxing. Trust me on this one."

She let out a chuckle while stroking Fluff's fur. "I'll give you that."

"What? I got the last word with boss lady. I should mark this on my calendar."

"Uh-uh, I'm not that bad."

"Let's just say you can be very persuasive."

"That's called leadership skills, my dear. Isn't that right, Fluff?"

He meowed again, followed by a purr as she scratched his ears.

"Of course he agrees with you. He's completely smitten." I moved over to the couch and took a seat on the end, hoping not to crowd her since she sat in the middle. "Hey, are you hungry? I can go down to the pizzeria on the corner and grab a couple of slices for us. We do have to figure out what to do with Fluff here."

"I think I'll need to sleep on it. I mean... I don't exactly have a lot of options. But I have thought of renting out an apartment just for him. You know, I could keep him there, and my sister wouldn't have to get monthly allergy shots. Or I could move into a bigger place, move my sister on one side of the place and him to another? Maybe I could put up a cat gate or something? Or... and this is my least favorite thing... we can find him a really good home. But I want to foster him. Maybe put him in a kennel so you don't have to deal? Something..." Geneva wasn't looking at me, and I knew she would go with whatever I said, but I did want to help her. It wouldn't be fair to an animal to have to deal with my mess, though.

I honestly heard her tossing out one bad idea after another and couldn't believe what my raggedy conscience came up with. "I think I have a solution. Let me talk to some friends, but I believe there are wonderful shelters that we can get him into. I can keep him until then." The common-sense side of my brain threw out everything I'd rationalized earlier—that I was going to walk away after the court case, that I was going to leave Geneva be so she didn't have to feel guilty about her job and starting a relationship with an intern, that I was nothing more than a common liar and she deserved better than that. But the hopeful side of my brain told old common sense to shut the fuck up. I recalled Dex telling me about the place he'd gotten his dog from, so I was hopeful they dealt with cats. I would check around for her, and as much as I loved helping Geneva, I didn't want to have to walk away from Fluff either at the end of the day.

"Mac... I know you are so kind, but I don't want to put you out. If..."

I could see the appreciation growing in her eyes, and it was honestly the best I'd felt about myself all day. "I'm not that put out. I think Fluff and I can come to an agreement. He can stay on his side of the room, and I'll stay on mine. Just until I find somewhere for him."

"This is the best news. I mean... I'm so grateful for you doing this." Without warning, she leaned over and threw both arms around my neck.

God help me, but she smelled so good, her skin felt so soft as I returned her embrace, and her curly hair, which she'd left down for the day, tickled under my nose. I could wake up with her hair in my face every day for the rest of my life. She was a treat to all my senses. I noticed and, inconveniently, so had my cock.

Damn it all, I was a goner.

# CHAPTER 18

## GENEVA CHAPMAN

*I* went back the next two mornings before work to see Fluff, and the next two nights too. Mac was awesome to let him stay, and part of me was sad it was all coming to an end since the shelter could take him soon. Sure, I enjoyed seeing Fluff, but I was growing more and more fond of Mac too. For a few hours every day, I could forget he was my intern and pretend we were some happy, dating couple. It was honestly working out better than expected. He hadn't asked me out again. At work, we were completely professional, and Cliff hadn't come at me about our working relationship anymore.

After a couple of days, though, I didn't want to push any more of Mac's boundaries, so I stayed away, vowing to return on the weekend. When he'd shared he couldn't keep Fluff, I'd been a teensy bit devastated, but I had to respect it. And... well, it was kind of nice to get a glimpse of resolute Mac. So, not visiting was more than just the boundary thing, when I thought about it. This was a precautionary measure. For my own safety. He was wearing on my resolve with his kindness, his attractiveness, and, my God, his body.

It was Friday, however, and Mac was going to present the security protocols to the senior leadership team, and that included Dex Truitt. I was nervous for him, but he didn't seem to mind—like at all.

"So... did you need me to review your presentation? I'm very good at transitional slide decks and graphics. Kind of my forte." I didn't want to look too desperate, but he sat across the desk from me, filling out his suit the way he did, and looked like the most confident, enigmatic professional in the world, despite my nervous pleas.

"No, I'm good. I practiced at home. Even got the Fluff seal of approval today. He rubbed his head on my leg when I was done."

"Oh, that is good. You know Fluff would never betray your confidence."

"Hee. I'm finding that out. Anyway, I'm gonna head over to the conference room to get things set up."

"Okay. And listen, I'll bring your laptop over to you when I come. I got this wireless remote for you to navigate the slide deck without touching your laptop. I just need to install it so you can get right into the meeting." I waved the remote to emphasize my helpfulness.

"Oh, that's cool. I didn't even think to do that. Let me grab it for you."

"Great."

In a flash, he was back with the laptop. "So, my password is BlackMagic674, in case it goes to sleep on you while installing. Capital B and M. Thanks again. I'll see you down there." Mac hit me with a warm smile, letting me know that he really did enjoy his job.

"Yup, see you in a few."

When he was gone, I installed the software and brought up the presentation to make sure I was able to navigate through the slide show. But... some of the slides had some grammar issues. So I changed those. Surely, he wouldn't mind a few edits. I hit save and checked the time. Perfect. I still had five minutes to spare.

I jogged down the hallway and found he was the only person in there. "Here you go. All set."

"Awesome. And hey, don't worry. I have always been pretty good at presentations. I don't expect this to go any differently."

"Me either. You'll be fine. I'm just always super nervous on my presentations."

"I don't understand why. You're very capable."

My heart warmed, and I could feel the blush come over me. That's when I heard it.

"Ahem. Good morning." Cliff's voice boomed into the room. Asshole.

"Morning, Cliff," I replied, then turned and walked away from Mac.

Cliff took a seat right in the center of the table. He looked as if he could incite a riot at any moment. Maybe that was just his face? He had changed so much from the friendly person I'd met my first day. Now he was colder, and almost mean-spirited. I guess you can never really know a person from a first impression.

Execs started to trickle into the room, and just five minutes before the start of the meeting, Dex Truitt arrived and closed the door behind him. He was the kind of person who commanded the room. Everyone around the table straightened a bit in their seats, including me. Everyone that is, except Mac. He seemed to have that same ease as he did in our office. Cliff cleared his throat again. All that, and you'd think he had the flu.

"Good morning, everyone. We're in for a treat today. Mac Berger..." he started, somehow making Mac's name sound like a slur. "Well, he's presenting us with this firewall integration program. And I guess we'll see how good it is. Take it away, Mac." He sat back in his seat looking like disgust, if disgust were a person.

"Thank you, Cliff." Mac smoothly turned in his chair and started the presentation. "As Cliff mentioned, I'm Mac Berger, and today, I'll show you what I've been working on these last couple of weeks throughout my internship, under Ms. Chapman's guidance. But let me take you back a beat to share what you had so you can clearly understand the improvements we've made."

Hmm, he was really good. He carried through all the programming changes, highlighting areas that had needed patches and system workarounds in the past, and was ready to guide us through the new system. "I don't mean to educate you on your software issues because you all know better than anyone the challenges you've had with your teams in the past. What I do intend to do is show you the exact areas where changes were needed. And here we are..." But when he hit the remote to advance the next slide, nothing happened. "Let's just try that once more." Still nothing. In fact, he closed the presentation and opened it again. There were no more slides after the last one he'd presented. "Well, it seems there's a glitch in my deck."

I hoped my face wasn't showing my concern. I knew the slides were there. I'd just seen them when I reviewed the deck and made the changes. Unless... oh my God...

My heart beat against my ribcage so hard I thought everyone in the room could hear it.

"Well, if you would open the folders in front of everyone's space, I took the liberty of making printouts. I believe we left off on slide twenty-five. If you could flip to that page, I'll proceed old-school." Everyone in the room laughed at his joke.

Everyone except Cliff. He looked even angrier than before.

Every question that came Mac's way, he answered with this flair. Confidence exuded from him and could only be defined as swagger. He was prepared for any difficulty, poised, funny, and engaging. I couldn't have been prouder of him. In fact, by the time he was done, I was outright giddy, even though I might've been the one to possibly cause the oops in the first place. I would let him know the moment I got a chance. I was sure he would understand.

I was the first to get up from my chair to walk over to him. "Oh, that was just great. You really are good at public speaking. Maybe you could mentor the mentor one of these days," I said, placing a hand on his forearm.

"I doubt you'd need it. You're probably better than you think." He gave me a smile, but before we could get into it, we both heard his name called. As Mac glanced around the room, I followed suit.

"Oh..." Mac said. "Mr. Truitt wants to see me. I'll see you at your office and you can tell me more about how great I am." He winked at me then was off to see the owner of Montague.

How amazing was that? I gathered up my things and headed out of the room, glancing over in their direction, where they were laughing and chatting, before leaving. Cliff pushed past me in a huff, and I followed him out.

I decided to catch up to him, though. It was time I got to the bottom of his disdain for Mac. If this continued, it could very well hinder Mac's future. What if Mr. Truitt wanted to offer him a job? Would Cliff stand in the way?

"Hey, Cliff, may I speak to you for a moment?"

With a sigh, he stopped and turned around. "Yes, Geneva." He leaned against the wall as if he'd grown tired just looking at me.

"I need to understand your disdain for Mac. I mean, he's a young man with a bright future. He did an amazing job in there, and it seemed it only pissed you off more. What's up, because somehow, this just doesn't feel normal. Even to me, and I've only been here a couple weeks." I tried to keep my voice down since we were in the middle of the hallway.

"I don't know. I guess I just don't trust him." Cliff loosened the knot of his tie. His lips were pressed thin as he stared back at me.

"I mean, didn't you pick him for the program?" I could feel my brows nearly touch.

"Yeah, I did," he said, blowing out a breath through partially closed, thin-as-hell lips. "I guess we can all make mistakes."

"Wow. So... if you had to recommend him to a job, would you? Even though he's doing a great job working for me?"

"No. To be honest, I would never recommend him to any job."

"And why is that?"

"Well, let's just say you can't believe everything you see. Now if you'll excuse me, I'm late for a lunch date with my wife to plan a surprise birthday party. And much as I rue planning events, I'd rather do that than spend another minute talking about Mac Berger."

Without giving me a chance to counter his hateful statements, he about-faced my ass, leaving me in the hallway to ponder what his last statement could have possibly meant.

The time had come. I would have to ask Mac if he knew anything about the reason Cliff didn't like him. Yeah, I was becoming bolder in my efforts to help him, but it was just because I knew he had a bright future, and one day, he would have to work with his own Cliff. If he did have something to do with the way Cliff felt, we'd need to address the issue head-on. As I walked back to my office, I resolved it was the only true way we could proceed if he wanted to work at Montague or any other organization and use his internship as a reference.

It was going to be a tough conversation, but not all things in life were pleasant. Of that much, I could attest.

## CHAPTER 19

## CALEB GREENE

"*Y*ou always were one to overdo it, weren't you?" Dex laughed in a hushed tone. Honestly, the only person besides Dex who knew my secret was Cliff, so he needed to keep it on the low.

"I mean, maybe. But that's how I've saved your ass countless times."

"Yeah, whatever. How's the cat?"

"Annoying as hell and greedy. Do you know how much wild-caught salmon cat food runs you?"

"No. I have a dog, man."

"A fucking lot. And despite me buying him the best cat mattress in the world, he prefers to sleep on my chest."

"Ah, man. The things we do for love. You any closer to telling her the truth?"

"No," I replied. I knew I was being snippy, but a part of me wanted to hang on just a little while longer, given her views on lying-ass men. "I'll tell her. I mean, the mediation is next week, so I'd better come up with something soon."

"Can't say I didn't warn you, man. You can't hide out here forever. You've got a company to run."

"Tell me something I don't know. Thing is, I don't really like the resolution."

"Okay, well, don't milk it. The sooner you come clean, the sooner you can see if your relationship has the mettle. Oh, and by the way, I'm keeping that security platform for all the trouble you've caused. Not giving you a penny either. Consider it payment for those soon-to-be million-dollar lofts."

"Like Manhattan needs more million-dollar lofts."

"Well, these are mixed-use. I'll be offering subsidies on the lower floors to address some of the housing issues for organizations in the area. Most of their employees can't afford to live near work, which causes more traffic, which causes greenhouse emissions."

"Wow, look at you, Mr. Greenspace. Consider the programming my gift to you for allowing me to meet her."

"Yeah, don't mention it. And don't tell anyone about my little project. Everyone thinks I'm a shark."

"Oh, your secret is safe with me. But if you'll excuse me, I need to get over to Geneva's office to get my well-deserved pat on the head, like any good intern worth their salt."

"You'd better tell her before that pat on the head becomes a kick in the ass."

"Touché, man. Catch you later. After the mediation."

"Well, good luck on that shit. And make sure you let me know what happens." Dex began to gather up his things from the table, but I couldn't wait to walk with him. I needed to get to Geneva.

As sad as it was, I wanted her to be proud of me. I was

back down the hallway in minutes. "Knock, knock," I said as I walked in.

"Oh my gosh, you are like a golden boy. What did Mr. Truitt say to you?" She was genuinely happy for me, positively beaming in my direction. If I were lucky enough to come home to that every day, I would never go to bed angry. I would treat Geneva like the queen she was.

"He just wanted to commend me on the work and ask a few questions about programming support. It was very nice of him, though."

"Indeed it was. Please have a seat. I have a couple of things to tell you."

I needed to sit, so I was glad she asked. First, she was wearing a white cotton dress, fitted through the waist and down to her knees. I could see her breathing in the thing, and I could barely contain myself. The whole day, I'd been sitting cross-legged in front of her. The other thing was, if she wanted to talk to me, she must not have been busy. It had been so long since we'd had an involved conversation in the daytime, I didn't know what to do with myself.

"Sure." I took the chair closest to her and crossed my legs again, damn my eager cock.

"So, I want to apologize. I think I may have corrupted your file when I was testing out the remote. And since you know I hate lying, I made a couple of edits to your slides. I think I may have lost the last portion of your work. I'm so, so sorry, and I shouldn't have messed with it in the first place since you asked me not to. But I wouldn't have felt right not saying anything to you. And thankfully," she said, extending her arms out, "you were so well prepared, you didn't miss a beat. I am truly sorry."

Damn, as irritating as it was to have someone mess

with my work—me being a perfectionist—how could I be angry with her for trying to help? "Oh... I mean, well, I understand. Your name is attached to my work too. I—I get it. Thank you for letting me know. I thought maybe I saved the wrong file or something."

"No, you didn't do anything wrong. I shouldn't have snooped, but I have shared in the past that I have a few control issues I'm working through."

"Don't even think of it. It's understandable, and as you said, I was prepared for any problems."

"Great. And now... there's something else. I need to ask, and I hope you don't think I'm prying, but what happened between you and Cliff? I've never seen anyone so bothered by someone. I thought it may have been related to prejudice, but his disdain for you feels almost personal. So, can you think back to your hire date and think of anything that could have happened, no matter how small?"

I knew why Cliff didn't like me. He detested that Dex was letting me carry out a farce at his workplace. He abhorred that I was taking advantage of a space intended for someone genuinely interested in working for Montague. He resented that I was using my friendship with Dex to hit on a woman. Which made him a decent guy, actually. "No... can't think of a thing."

"It's just so weird. You know? He's a pragmatic man who is pretty level-headed... I just don't get it. It's disturbing."

As she spoke, I was thinking of all the things she'd told me. When she jacked up my slide deck, she shared with me what she'd possibly done and apologized, even though I may have never known her involvement. She was decent too. Dex was apparently great at finding honest talent. I wondered if anyone at my own company was as upstanding as Cliff and Geneva were. "Yes, it is. I honestly can't think of why."

"Well, I'm unnerved enough to take this up the chain. I think I'm going to talk to Mr. Truitt about his treatment of you. I don't want his actions to impact you, and who knows if he would flip the script on some other intern. I know how hard you've worked, and I don't want that compromised by someone who is obviously biased against you."

*Oh, fuck no.* I couldn't let her do that. I promised Dex I wouldn't cause issues at his company. Hell, I wasn't even an employee, and to have her angry at the man over a bull-shit game I was playing wasn't fair—to Geneva or to Cliff. "Wait, I... I think there may be a reason, but Geneva... I don't want to share on company property."

"Oh... was it— Was it something really bad?"

"I mean, it depends on how you look at it. When I tell you, though, I want you to be on neutral ground. I don't want whatever we discuss to upset you while you're at work. And please" —I held my hands up, practically begging her to consider holding off talking to Dex—"don't do anything before you talk to me."

"I guess I can hold off. When do you want to talk about it? I would prefer it be sooner rather than later. I'm a little concerned now." She did look anxious. She worried at her lower lip as she waited for me to respond, her doe-shaped eyes wide with apprehension.

"We can do it tonight."

"I can't tonight. I promised my sister I'd come home. She texted a little while ago and said she had something exciting to share. I don't want to bail on her. How about tomorrow afternoon?"

"Anytime you're free, I'll make it work for you." I knew the last statement was a stretch. Who knows, after I told her what I had to say, she may kick my ass. I would honestly deserve it. I'd been so unfair to her the last few weeks by not telling her the truth. I'd taken advantage of her, mostly because the opportunity had presented itself. And she was not the type of person who needed someone to lie to her.

"Great. I'll text you before I leave my house in case Fluff needs something."

"Oh, trust me. That cat has everything he'll ever need. I'm pretty sure he thinks I'm the maître d' around that place."

"Well, aren't you? Glad you finally figured out his favorite cat food. I thought he was going to go on a starvation strike."

"It was touch-and-go for a while. I was sleeping with one eye open."

"Honestly, I don't blame you."

We both laughed for a while, peppered with me telling her what she'd missed in the last few nights and fighting hard not to tell her how much I missed her.

I convinced Geneva to take a walk with me to pick up some food, and we were on the street when some of the guilt I'd been carrying around with me over all my lies eased a bit from our relaxed conversation. If everything came out on Saturday and she didn't forgive me, this may very well be our last meal together. I needed to make the most of it, despite the worsening fear that it would soon all be over. "What's on the menu today?"

"Oh, I don't know. I think I'm in the mood for ice cream. There's a great one over by Jorge's truck in Bryant Park. Should be the day for it. It's Friday and a thousand degrees today." Geneva pulled at her sleeves, opening the buttons at the wrist. "You know, I wish the AC wasn't set to freezing in the building. Maybe I could wear short sleeves every now and again. Now that you and Dex are buddies, can you put in a good word for that?"

"Oh, you got jokes, I see."

"I mean, y'all talked for a while." She laughed, sprinting across the street with the other pedestrians.

Naturally, I followed right behind her, and we cut through the cars stuck between traffic lights. "We did. I would have been remiss if I didn't tell him how grateful I was to be on your team. I don't know, maybe you have an in with him yourself."

"Please. I'm one of forty directors around that place. I don't think Mr. Truitt has a minute on his hands."

"Yeah well... I'll see what I can do about the AC."

"Much appreciated."

As we continued our brisk walk to Brenna's Ice Cream Stand, I watched her. The way she moved, the breaths she took, her free spirit embodied in her light gait and wistful hair. Geneva was everything I wanted and needed.

# CHAPTER 20

## GENEVA CHAPMAN

*A*s I arrived home that day, I considered texting Mac to tell him I'd be over after speaking with Leddie. As long as what she had to tell me wasn't bad, I could possibly go see him and Fluff. It was probably time I stopped using Fluff as an excuse too. I enjoyed my time with Mac, and while I certainly couldn't have a sexual relationship with him while he reported to me, I could maybe see what shook out after his internship was done. Perhaps he wouldn't even want to work at Montague. Maybe... There were so many reasons to be hopeful, but mostly *he* was the reason. He was so kind and forgiving.

I probably needed to work on that myself. For so long, I'd expected every man to treat me like my father had treated my mom. He used her love to stay in her life even though he had gambling addictions. If he had sought help, maybe he wouldn't have been the man he was. And maybe their life would have turned out differently. Even if it hadn't, they could have been happy when they died together. Their lives were too short to be so miserable. My time with Mac made me see all these things. But it didn't hurt like it usually did. Mac helped me come to the realization that sometimes things just work out as they should. With or without my help.

I unlocked the door and stepped inside the apartment. I could smell tomato sauce on the stove. "Leddie, are you cooking?" I knew I hadn't made anything before I left, and there was nothing in the freezer that could have smelled that good.

"Hey, I'm in here. And yes, I'm making us dinner."

I stepped into the kitchen and saw Leddie propped up on a tall stool, stirring something in a pot. "What are you doing?" I shrieked. I thought of all the things that could go wrong in that setup. She could fall or pull the hot pot over onto herself. "You shouldn't be doing that."

"Relax, girl. I cook for myself all the time."

"Why?" I asked, feeling more than a little stupid. How long had I been treating Leddie like a child?

"Sometimes, I want something other than what you made. But today we're celebrating. I wanted to make *you* something for a change. Besides, you worked all day."

"What do you mean you cook?"

"Yeah, of course I cook. I never understood why you thought if you didn't make me something to eat, I'd starve. But girl, I'm handi-capable. I can do anything you can do. I don't want to talk about that, though. Go change and come back. I have news."

I never understood the word flabbergasted. It was an extremely long-winded way of saying shocked, but sometimes, shocked wouldn't do. When I saw Leddie at the stove cooking, I had to admit, I moved past shocked straight into flabbergasted territory. More to do with the fact that I'd missed her moving past the needing-me stage.

She was a grown-ass woman... I would need to learn to respect that.

I did as she said, though. I went into my bedroom and put on a gray T-shirt and some of my favorite ripped jeans before emerging to find the table set and a steaming hot bowl of spaghetti with salad and garlic bread in the middle. "All right," I said, taking my seat. "What's all this about? And it better be worth you giving me a heart attack when I walked in."

"Girl, you know you have to have things your way all the time. Cooking is something you seem to like doing. I let you do it. It gave you joy, and honestly, since you spent most of your life making sure I had everything I needed, I didn't mind you taking care of me."

A pang of remorse went through my chest, along with a bit of pride. I don't believe I'd ever given Leddie the benefit of the doubt. "Well, now I know." I struggled to keep my chin from quivering. "And I'm sorry for that. I shouldn't have underestimated you." I fought back the tears in my eyes, not knowing whether I should say more.

Leddie tossed me a wink with a broad smile. "Start eating, girl. This is one of my best dishes."

When Leddie picked up a plate and started heaping food onto it, I knew she was doing her best to show me my apology was accepted. "But I have a question."

"Yup." She finished the first dish, then brought it down to my end in the wheelchair.

"Thank you," I said, accepting the plate. "Why didn't you ever clean my room since you're super capable?"

I snickered as she leveled a death glare on me.

"I said I'm handi-capable, not Wonder Woman. It'll take a miracle to clean your room, and I'm not here for it."

She laughed as she fixed her own plate and took it back to her space.

"So, you're going to make me wait until we're done with dinner to tell me your news? I almost ran here from the subway. And hurry up, because I have something to tell you too." I took a heaping bite and had to stop myself from moaning. "Oh, this is good," I said, pointing at the food.

"Oh, that's right." Leddie feigned absentmindedness, placing a hand on her head. "Wherever did I put the paperwork?"

"Girl, quit playing with me."

"Fine, party pooper." She wheeled herself over to the coffee table and pick up a packet, placed it on her lap, and brought it back to me. "Here. I'm balling out of control, girl. Wait 'til you see." She clapped her hands together after I took the envelope from her.

I laid it on the table beside my plate and opened it to see... Mac. Not like regular Mac. This Mac was poised in a black suit with gold cufflinks. This Mac smiled at the camera and projected an image of confident businessman. He wasn't down to earth or a germaphobe, and he for damned sure didn't live in a fucked-up warehouse nearly on the outskirts of Manhattan.

"Caleb Greene and AppTech accepted *Flowerville*. Can you believe that?" She practically squealed while telling me. And all the blood in my body seemed to rush through my ears.

Hurt didn't even begin to describe the cavernous hole in my chest. "Excuse me... what did you call him?"

"That's Caleb Greene. He's going to fund my app. Isn't this exciting?"

I didn't want to crush my sister's dreams. Nor did I

want to let on that the man whose picture was shown in the *About Us* section of the packet had been intimate with me on more than one occasion—not sex, but intimate. He'd shared things with me and comforted me, and for fuck's sake, he was taking care of my cat. "Oh, um... that's really great, Leddie."

"Well, I'm sure he didn't write this. Probably just some admin, but he called *Flowerville* innovative and fresh. He's a mogul, so that's quite a compliment..."

I couldn't say anything. I stared back into those warm eyes, the same eyes that let me cry on his shoulder and told me the world would be ours if we made it. If "we" made it... Who the hell is *we* if he's a millionaire? And what did he think? That I was some kind of gold digger? Some charity case he couldn't trust to not abuse him and his wealth? Or was the intent to sleep with the "help"? I'd heard before that powerful men would play all sorts of games with women. I couldn't very well say he wasn't that type of person since he'd been spouting bullshit since the day I met him.

I wanted to be angry. Instead, I was just hurt. My heart clenched in my chest, even if I was so incredibly happy for my sister. I wanted to tell her "fuck that guy," but how could I rain on the happiest news we'd had since before our parents died? A few hours ago, that would have been me over her acceptance with AppTech. But I didn't even know if she'd gotten it on her own merit or if Mac... or Caleb, whatever the fuck his name was, had somehow found out she'd submitted and gave it to her to continue this messed-up-ass game.

"Well, say something..." Leddie brought me back to the now with her words. When I looked at her again, her head was tilted with a puzzled look on her face.

"Oh, yeah. That's a great compliment."

"Okay, what's going on? I mentioned the compliment a while ago. You aren't even listening."

"Nothing... I'm just so happy for you." I got up from the table and walked around her, heading toward the living room.

"You don't look happy. Is everything okay at work?"

"Yeah, I mean... I had a thing with a guy at work, but that's all good now... I guess." What if Cliff had known, and that's why he didn't like Mac? And he'd tried to tell me, damned fool that I was.

"Then what? You seem shook."

I should have known not to try keeping anything from her. She was my sister and my best friend. There was no way she wouldn't notice if my world was shattering. So, I leaned into something she knew well about me. Worry. "It's just, I know you'll probably be moving out of here soon. I was thinking about what I would do when that day came." A total lie, but it sounded plausible.

"Oh, Gigi." The whir of her wheelchair turning to face me brought my head up. When I looked at her, there were tears twinkling in her eyes. "I will never be too far away. You're my rock. And it's okay to feel that way. When I heard you on the phone with Mac, I thought the exact same thing."

Fuck. I'd almost forgotten she knew about him. Well, she would never meet him, so no harm, no foul. But then... I thought about it. Thought about what I was doing to my relationship with my sister. The one who was actually important.

I stepped away from Leddie, my heart dropping steadily to my feet as I made my way to the couch. "I can't do this..." I was set to go. I intended to lie to Leddie so she wouldn't see me break. For so long, I'd been her comforter, always hiding my fear, my failures, so I could be there for her. For the first time, I was seeing her for who she was truly. I needed to let her see me too.

"Can't do what?" I heard her chair moving over the carpet as she followed me. Concern evident in her voice.

"I..." I fell onto the couch and held my head in my hands. "I can't lie to you. Not like he's done to me."

"Ok..." I could hear something hard hit and realized it was probably her slapping the arm of her wheelchair. "You'd better tell me something before I lose it. Did someone hurt you?"

I could barely stand to look at her, but I did. I didn't want her to see the pain in my eyes. "Mac... Caleb... whatever the fuck. He lied to me. That guy in the picture," I said, pointing to her desk, "he's my intern. He's Mac Berger."

"Mac Berger is his name, and you didn't think that was made up?"

"People have weird names all the time. I didn't think anything of it. But now that you've pointed it out, I feel extra dumb."

"Oh, Gigi. I apologize. Humor is my defense mechanism when I'm ready to hunt someone down."

"Oh no... no... I shouldn't have trusted him. I shouldn't have let him in. I don't even know why I'm so hurt. I was the one who lectured him about boundaries, after all..." The heat of fresh tears left a trail down my cheeks. In an instant, it was as if all the strength drained from me. Hurt didn't even begin to describe the cavernous hole in my chest. It had been a long time, what felt like decades, since I'd cried so hard.

"I'm so sorry." Leddie held her arms wide, and

instinctively, I moved to the end of the couch and allowed her to cradle me. More tears fell in an unstoppable torrent. But I needed it. So, I stayed there, my head on her shoulder, her hand gently stroking my back as I quaked with sobs.

It had been an eternity since I'd leaned on my sister. Or anyone other than Caleb. I still wanted to call him Mac, but that guy was gone. Dead.

I needed to talk to him, but what good would it do? There was nothing to make me forgive him for fucking with me. For lying to me about who he was.

Here lies Caleb Greene. The last man who would ever make a fool of me again.

# CHAPTER 21

## CALEB GREENE

*I* was going to kill him later. Mac was no more. It was absolutely time to tell Geneva who I was. With one more day of mediation in front of me, and being perilously close to losing my company, she was bound to find out from the press. My picture would be splashed all over the *Wall Street Journal* once the news was out. With the last text Owenthal had sent, I knew Blain was going to take the gloves off. He had pics of me in various compromised positions with a number of women. I didn't even recall dating them. He must have had me under surveillance for a while. Normally, that would not have done it for me. I didn't give a shit about being seen with women. What I cared about was not adding more reasons for Geneva to hate me. Add being a man-whore on top of a mountain of lies, and I would for sure come out smelling not remotely like a rose.

I regretted not saving my company, but not a minute of the time spent over the last week. I really liked—okay, *liked* was too soft of a descriptor for what I felt—I *loved*

Geneva. She was so thoroughly integrated into my life, I don't even know how the hell I lived before.

*Now, if she'll just answer the damn phone.* I'd been calling her for hours. And texting. I'd even sent her a picture of Fluff with a caption that read "missing you." Sure, she could ignore me, but how could she not respond to the furball? It wasn't like her.

Since it was after noon on Saturday, I was starting to wonder if something had happened. I glanced around one last time, looking for anything that could have been out of place. The scene was perfect. I'd bought food from the food truck we'd first gone to, her favorite flowers, her favorite song cued up on repeat...

I don't know what I thought she would say. I'd lied to her about my identity. I needed to make it good, and make sure she knew how I felt.

When my phone rang, I nearly jumped out of my skin. I'd been so lost in thought, I'd almost lost track of the time. I picked up the phone, relieved to find my waiting was over. "Geneva, I thought you'd lost your phone."

"Nope."

I couldn't help but notice the ice in her voice. "I um— I called you. And the furball insisted we call."

"I've been busy. With my sister."

"Oh, are you still able to make our plans?"

"Yup. Wouldn't miss it for the fucking world."

Despite her words, her tone belied their meaning. "O-okay. What time will you be by?"

"Give me a few minutes and I'll get an Uber."

"Great. I can't wait to see you. There are some things I need to talk to you about. It's time." Instead of her reply, I caught the telltale three tones of an ended call.

Now, I was pacing. There was something going on,

but was it narcissistic to think it had anything to do with me? That line from "You're So Vain" played in my mind. The song is older than me, but still so goddamn relevant.

By the time she arrived, I'd reheated the food and put the final touches on the warehouse space for the third time. It couldn't be perfect enough for what I needed to say and how I needed to say it. It had to be loaded with sincerity and completely honest. More honest than I'd ever been.

The elevator arrived, and I was waiting right there for her, having heard the movement of the pulley shift into action.

Fluff leapt into my arms, probably to give me some added support. He could perhaps sense how nervous I was. Another thing I would have to thank Geneva for.

"Hey, boss lady." I greeted her with a huge smile as I stroked the furball.

"Um-hmm."

Okay, not the greeting I'd expected, but as she passed me, she scratched Fluff between the ears, to which he purred.

"Okay, I know I was a little sketchy yesterday, but I have to tell you why. And before I do, I want you to try and have an op—"

I'd been following her from the makeshift foyer into the belly of the loft when she whirled on me. "Who are you?"

A wave of sweat coated my skin instantly. There was fire in her eyes as she narrowed them and trained them in my direction.

"What?" I'd clearly been shocked stupid by her aggression, her fury. I could feel it radiating from her.

"You heard me. I asked, who are you? I'm not even

sure why when I can Google you and get your company name, your net worth, and oh... your name too, Caleb."

Fuck. My mother used to tell me to follow my first mind. Damned if she wasn't right again. "I can explain..."

"Do you realize how cliché that is? Of course you can explain. And it will be some self-serving reason which plays you up to be some heroic person, and me... the fool you played."

"I swear... it wasn't you. It's all my fault. But I didn't expect it to go this far."

"You didn't expect me to find out, you mean. You're sorry you got caught is what it sounds like."

"Can we sit down for a second?" I made a move toward her, but she shrank away. Like she didn't trust me anymore.

"No," she said. Her arms windmilled backward as she bumped the edge of the bed. She seemed to steady herself then by closing her eyes and taking a deep breath. "Don't do that... I won't accept that. I only came to confront you in person. To see if you were going to lie in my face again, *Caleb*." The words were tipped in venom, especially my real name.

"I just want to tell you how all this happened. I was being sued, and I thought you wouldn't like me anymore if you heard what I was being accused of."

"You sure you weren't just trying to protect your assets? A poor girl like me could be a liability. You know, you wouldn't want to jeopardize one of those millions, would you?"

"I don't have millions anymore. That's just it. I've been accused of stealing my ex-partner's ideas. We're in mediation, and right now, it looks like I won't have a dime left. I couldn't tell anyone, or else I would have been in violation of our mediation agreement. The terms *I* set. Don't you understand?"

"Then why did you even talk to me? You approached me with a straight-up lie. And now look at me. I'm a mess. This is the very last thing I need right now. I'm on the verge of getting my life together for the first time, and you pull this? I asked you not to break me, Mac... fuck, Caleb."

I couldn't help the lunge I made toward her, and for a moment, the sweetest moment of my entire life, I held her. Wrapped in my arms, her body quaked with sobs. Until she broke away. The moment she did, I was hit with a wave of darkness. Every cell in my body seemed to reach for her. The singular moment left me empty. Broken. Hell, she wasn't even gone... yet.

"Don't touch me. You're a liar, and there isn't a part of me that doesn't feel that betrayal. You're an asshole, just like every other rich dude in the world. You're everything they say you are. You just take, if for no other reason than knowing you can."

"Don't say that. It's not true." Her words cut to the bone. I knew she wasn't going to forgive me, but nothing was worse than her thinking I was shit. Fluff curled around her legs, like even he was taking her side. "Are you going to let me explain? At least give me that."

"I don't have to give you a damn thing. I'm done being played. I shared everything with you, and you couldn't even give me your name. You should have just had sex with me that night when I was drunk and spared me the agony of this." Geneva went from ten to zero, and I didn't know which was worse—the rage or the silence. She stood there for a moment, hand clutched to her chest. Her face was turned away from me, almost as if she couldn't bear to even look at me. And it tore my heart out.

"I did this to get close to you, yes. But it was never about sex. You made me feel free. I was going to tell you tonight."

"Isn't that what liars say? I was going to? I was going to leave my wife, I was going to stop cheating, I was going to keep you safe from a horrible fucking accident. A lie is a lie, Caleb. And you are a lying-ass man. Now, if you'll excuse me, I have to get back to my real life. That's if your buddy doesn't snatch away my job."

"I'm not your father, Geneva."

"Yeah? Well, at least he had the decency to keep his lies straight. He was one of the best. If he were alive, I'd introduce you two. You have a lot in fucking common. I'm out, Caleb. I can't take any more of this... my heart can't." She stormed past me, ripped the cage up, and stepped in before slamming it down again.

I wanted to stop her. To catch her and wipe the tears away, but something told me she was done. I had gambled with her trust and lost.

I watched as the lift took her down—the hurt and pain in her eyes would haunt me for the rest of my life. Along with the knowledge that I'd lost the best thing to ever happen to me.

# CHAPTER 22

## GENEVA CHAPMAN

*C*aleb didn't show up on Monday. Figures. His rich ass had taken an opportunity from someone who probably needed it. I didn't even know why I expected he would.

I couldn't believe I'd fallen for his shit. I'd spent the weekend crying while ignoring his calls and trying to keep up a brave face. I didn't want to admit how quickly I'd fallen for someone despite so many signs being there. And Cliff... oh my God, I didn't even want to think about how poorly I'd treated him on behalf of such a lowdown little shit as *Caleb Greene* turned out to be.

Caleb wouldn't know anything about how I'd spent the weekend. It didn't keep my traitorous heart from breaking into a million pieces. But I had things to do and people to speak to.

I made it upstairs to Dex Truitt's office in what seemed like seconds. Here I was, the first real conversation I was having with the man, and I was about to confront him about Caleb. How had he gotten into the company? It couldn't have been without anyone's knowledge. Given they'd seemed so chummy before, I knew the reason... now. The whole game had been orchestrated from the top.

I walked past his secretary's desk since no one was there and tapped on the glass of the open door.

He looked up at me, his shrewd eyes giving me a hint he already knew why I was there. "Ms. Chapman. Please, come in."

"Thank you." I didn't say anything else as I made my way across the room. I'd practiced my speech, and I didn't want to blow my opportunity to ask questions like I had with MacCaleb, which Leddie, with her shady self, had taken to calling him. "Good morning," I said, taking my seat.

"Morning. How can I help you?" He sat back in his seat and steepled his fingers.

"I need to know why you assigned Caleb Greene to my team."

As I expected, he didn't seem surprised. In one fluid movement, he sat forward and held my stare. "Because he was nuts about you and going through a rough time. To be fair, I warned him repeatedly that you were going to find out and he would have to deal with the repercussions. But please know, I do not make it a practice to do things like this. And given the outcome, I regret my choices. Ms. Chapman, I have made poor decisions in my life." With a shrug, he straightened in his chair again. "I do have regrets. Would I do it again if he asked me? Probably."

"Well, that's unfortunate. I would have expected you to say no," I said. I could feel my heart pounding in my chest. The thought crossed my mind—how many times had Caleb abused his power to meet women?

"I would do it again because when a man lacks

impulse control, loses the ability to rationalize, and is so consumed with meeting a woman that he poses as someone else, I know nobody can stop them. I knew the day you met him, Ms. Chapman—"

"Please, call me Geneva," I said with a sigh.

"Geneva, he was a lost cause."

"Is that a fact?"

"It is. Caleb is a Monk-level germaphobe. He told me he had lunch with you at a food truck. Do you know he thinks people pee in bottles in food trucks?"

"He shared that."

"He got on a subway. He climbed through a dumpster... Now, I am not asking you to forgive him, because frankly, I would be hurt and upset as well. But I at least wanted you to know where he was coming from. And if you never see him again, just know, he is not the terrible person you believe him to be."

I just sat there. Whatever I thought I was going to hear wasn't *that*. I thought there was going to be some kind of smoke and mirrors. A guy talking up his friend and not owning their part in the whole thing. But that wasn't what this was like at all.

"So, I promise you, I don't believe he intended for this to turn out this way. Even though I warned him. You should probably know he was about to tell you the truth... you just beat him to the punch."

"I found out from my sister." It was all I could manage because I was fighting hard to keep the tears from falling. Talking only made it worse.

"Yeah... figures. It's never a good idea to lie." I could agree with him there. "That being said, I am truly sorry for my part in the matter. I probably should have tried to stop him. I just didn't want to see him running around the five boroughs trying to find you. He had enough on his plate. I hope..." Dex rubbed a hand through his hair and leaned back. "I am hopeful you will stay on at Montague. Cliff tells me you're an outstanding employee. I think you'll do great things here."

"I... I hope to stay on. I just didn't know if this affected my empl—"

"Never. I am not a man to do things I don't want to do. You worked hard through your internship, and you earned the right to be here. I think you have a bright future here, Geneva."

It was my turn to be uncomfortable. I didn't want to leave. All in all, it was a great job with great people. Besides that, I wasn't ready to run away from a place just because of a man. I had to be stronger than that. "I think I would like to stay."

"Good. I'm glad. Now, I am sorry, but I have to run out to meet my wife, Bianca. She's hosting a charity event tonight, and I need to be her errand boy."

"Of course," I said, standing to leave. I attempted a smile but was sure it landed on my face as a weak grimace.

"And Geneva, I meant everything I said. About the job... and about Caleb."

I glanced back at Dex and knew his words were true. I just didn't know for sure if I could ever see Caleb the way he saw him. "Thank you."

I WAS OVER ALL OF IT BY LUNCH. I HAD TOO MUCH ON my mind, from all the things Dex had told me to looking up every few minutes half expecting to see Caleb. How had he infiltrated my life in such a short time? I felt like a world-class idiot. As soon as noon hit, I was out the door.

I went to Jorge's taco truck and stood in the long line to place my regular order. When I got there, he was all smiles as usual. "Hola, Mami."

"Hi there, my friend. I'll take a veggie burrito and some churros, please."

Despite the long line behind me, Jorge paused and tipped his head while he observed me. "You okay?"

"Yeah, just life stuff."

"I'm a nosy man, G. I think there's more to what you are saying. Does it have something to do with your friend, the tall one?"

I opened my mouth to say *I'm fine,* but instead, I nodded, blinking hard to clear tears from my eyes. When that didn't work, I swiped at them with my fingers.

Jorge offered me a tissue. "You know, I thought something was wrong when he tracked me down on a Saturday to get your usual. I was happy to help, but when he did it, I said to myself, 'there's one man who has some making up to do.'"

"He did what?" I almost couldn't believe my ears. "But you don't work on weekends."

"Yeah, that's what I told him. But he covered the cost of the meals for the homeless at St. Mary's for the next month. All to get you your favorite meal. It was a kind gesture, and I was able to feed more people. It was the least I could do for a nice man like that. So, I ask you... you sure there's no going back?"

My heart clenched, a warm sensation filling me, despite my wanting it to remain iced over. "I... I don't know. He lied to me, Jorge..."

"I remember when I lied to my Maria. It took a long

174

time. But eventually, she forgave me. I'm not telling you to forgive him, but sometimes, if you listen to his side, you may come to understand. And you're too pretty to be crying like this, Mami."

I wiped my eyes again since they were leaking. Over my shoulder, I heard the agitated moan. "Aye, Jorge, I gotta get back to work. Any day now."

Jorge looked up to find whoever was complaining and waved his hand. "One person at a time, Marquis." Shaking his head, he returned his attention to me. "All right, honey, these people are going to start a riot if I don't get moving. Just think about what I said. If it's worth anything, everything will work out. If not, keep that bit of info in your pocket to use next time."

"I will. And *gracias*." I handed him the cash to cover my meal.

"*De nada*. Step right down there, and Maria will get your food out."

Once he handed me the change, I shoved it in the tip jar. I should have paid him a bit more for the therapy he'd just given me. A part of me, though, wasn't ready. I needed to think about whether or not I wanted to hear Caleb's excuses.

His words bounced around in my mind. *I'm not your father, Geneva.*

Was I holding him responsible for all my father had done to my mother? My father had been a grifter, true. But his lies weren't the cause of their accident. His lies didn't take them away from me. The actual reason was distracted driving. I had no reason to believe lies were the cause, but in my mind, ever since my aunt told me my parents' truth, I'd believed he was at fault for taking her from me. In reality, I'd never forgiven my father.

Maria handed me the food and gave me a rush of kindnesses in Spanish. I smiled and nodded before bidding her goodbye. Maybe she would never care that I spoke terrible Spanish. I certainly accepted her compassion even if I didn't understand her fully.

I walked back to the Montague entrance and took my seat, digging into the burrito and savoring the spicy seasonings, thinking about my life and whether or not I'd possibly doomed my relationship with Caleb, and every other man, because I didn't want to end up like my mother.

There was no way I was going to let him slide for the lie, but I also didn't want to not hear him out. Jorge was right. Leddie had been right. And ultimately, when Caleb told me he wasn't Dad, he'd been right too.

Shit... I really hated being wrong about any of this.

# CHAPTER 23

## CALEB GREENE

*T*he day had been a shit show. As I sat before the mediator and Blain on Zoom, I imagined giving him a punch in his smug face. I was even angrier than before, even if it had nothing to do with the mediation hearing. I was still mad about my conversation with Geneva. Yeah, I was dead-ass wrong for lying, but I hadn't expected her not to listen to me at all. The anger wasn't even directed at her. It was aimed at everything else. Traffic, the blazing sun in the sky, and at the moment, Blain.

"In closing, Mr. Greene, we would like fifty percent of your share of AppTech. It is the EverType software that put your company on the map, after all. Without it, you would still be at the gate and begging venture capitalists for start-up capital."

Owenthal cleared his throat. "This is a harsh statement, considering your client stole classified documents and leaked them on the dark web the day before the product launched. Not to mention, there's a little thing called intellectual property."

"Not when they were partners. He cut my client out

of the business before launching an IPO. His stock would have been worth millions. Surely, you don't expect him to walk away from that."

"That's exactly what I expect him to do. If he can build a better app, then he should." Owenthal's elbows were pressed into the table so hard, it wobbled a bit.

The lawyers continued to snipe away, breaking down one another's logic until there was nothing left. Meanwhile, I was looking at Blain. He was tired, drawn. He was merely a broken version of the man he once was. As was I.

For the first time, I empathized with him. I felt terrible for the way things ended with Blain. True enough, I let him walk away knowing we were going to apply for an IPO. I had omitted information that could have made him change his mind about leaving, and all because of my pride. It wasn't right. Just like I'd done to Geneva. I didn't give her enough information to make a legitimate decision about a relationship.

*A lie is a lie...*

The words had stabbed at me, but she was right for the most part.

"What do you want, Blain?" I asked the question, and everyone onscreen seemed to focus on me.

"Mr. Greene, we are in the middle of mediation. The time to ask what he wanted would have been before you swindled him out of his half," his attorney sniped.

"Objection. You are not going to call him a common thief. Unlike your client," Owenthal countered.

"What do you want?" I asked again.

"Well, how about we start with what I don't want." Blain's steel gaze bored into me. "I don't want to have to start a new company from the ground up. I don't want to have software out there that I can't leverage as my work. I don't want to wake up every single day hating the day I lost everything because of you."

The gravity of his emotions hit differently for some reason. I hadn't heard anything he'd said before that moment. Ever since the day he'd stormed out of my office, I had shut Daniel down and refused to hear his side. He'd suffered for my actions. He didn't deserve that.

"I'm willing to give you seventy-five percent of the original business at its current value. It far exceeds your request. I think you will find it suitable to start your own company." Was it a snap decision? Hell, yeah. But hadn't it been the same when I sent him out on his own without any access to his software?

Everyone in the room dropped their jaws. I ignored them, instead tapping the amount out into the text message and sending it to the three of them. Then, the only one pissed was Owenthal.

"I don't have to tell you I think this is a bad idea, Caleb." His brows were cast so low, they looked like part of his cheeks. I didn't care. To be honest, nothing was worth having if you'd lied and cheated your way to the top. It was probably what had been bothering me the whole time.

I only glanced at him. I returned my attention to Daniel, ignoring Owenthal instead of wasting my breath. "I should have never done that to you. It wasn't fair. I profited from your ignorance in the situation, and you may never be able to forgive me for that. I don't know if I could, but I hope this makes up for it."

"I don't know what to say..." Daniel looked from me to his own attorney, who was speechless as well.

"You don't have to say anything. I trust you all can

write this up and make sure everything is set to transfer. If I had a checkbook, I would write it out right now."

"Thank you, Caleb. I appreciate you for doing this. It's way more than I imagined."

"Yeah, my stock will take a hit at the next quarterly meeting, but that's why we continue developing, isn't it? I'll be fine. Now, you will too."

"Mr. Greene, I'll get the papers over to you both in the morning. Would you like them sent to your hotel or to your office in California?"

"Not sure. I'll let you guys know later tonight." I honestly didn't know if I had anything left to save in New York. But I didn't want to leave without giving it one more shot. Maybe when she calmed down... No, she didn't need to calm down. It was notions like that one that made men so infuriating. My mistake wasn't on her. It was on me.

I got up from the table and left without a word more to the trio. I would pay Owenthal well for his help since I'd probably given him a coronary with that figure, but I would compensate him. All of his advice was what I'd wanted. Before I changed. Now, I needed to fix one more thing before it was too late.

## CHAPTER 24

### GENEVA CHAPMAN

"*G*eneva, are you ready to talk about this yet?" Leddie exclaimed.

I didn't blame her for using my government name, especially since I'd been moping around for a few days. "I haven't talked about it because I don't want to rain on your parade."

"Raining on my parade is slapping an ice cream cone out of my hand. This is some asshole hurting my sister. How do we know he didn't just award me the contract because I'm your sister? That isn't fair to me and the team. *Flowerville* is a damn good game."

Another knife speared at me. I didn't want Leddie to start doubting her creativity and all the work that had gone into her game. "No... no, he didn't do that. I don't even think his mind has been on the grant competition. He's been running around here pretending to be someone else, and according to him, dealing with a lawsuit that could take his company from him. So, your app is awesome. Don't ever think it's anything other than what it is. Fantastic. The mess with Caleb and me... that's just between us. Not anything to do with you or *Flowerville*."

The last comment sent Leddie wheeling back and forth across the length of the living room. I could tell from the red splotches on her chest and cheeks she was angry. She always lit up like a Christmas tree when she was pissed. "I have half a mind to send his ass a sternly worded email." She was so upset, she used her wheels to roll her instead of the controls. Another sign she was blowing off steam.

"Well, be sure to put best wishes on the end, that way, he'll know you mean business."

Leddie stopped her to and fro to level me with a glare. Then, she laughed, which was what I was aiming for. "You really know how to take the wind out of a sail, don't you?"

"I know. But I honestly don't want you throwing away your dream over me. The game is brilliant. Take the money. Build the platform you need, then take over the world. Caleb hurt me, but there's no reason for you to suffer. You deserve this. You know, despite all this extra crap, I really am proud of you."

Leddie smiled, and it was like taking a step back in time. The way her eyes lit up, I could see Mom. "Thanks, sis."

I walked over to her and kneeled in front of her chair, clasping a hand over her knee. "You're welcome. Now, go tell your team. They're dying to know."

Leddie placed a warm hand over mine, then leaned forward to kiss me on the forehead. "If you need me to roll down on him, just let me know." Some words were more terrifying when whispered. My sister had just proven that.

"I will." I rose slightly to return the gesture, planting my lips on her temple before rising fully. I needed to get out of the room. All her sentimental talk had got me in the chest, and the warm sensation formed a knot in my throat. I blinked hard to clear the tears that had yet to fall and hightailed it down the hallway and into my bedroom. I threw myself onto the bed, pulling one of my decorative pillows to my face, and finally allowed the waterworks to start. Warm and salty, my tears spilled over my cheeks and down my neck into my hair. I had no idea when they would stop, but I didn't have the energy to hold them back.

Despite my earlier resolution that I should have given him a chance to explain himself, I wasn't ready to call him. I wasn't even sure we should be together. When a relationship started under false pretenses, how was I to know it was real? How could I be sure he was real?

I don't know how long it was before a notification went off on my phone. Then again, and another in a few seconds, the incessant pings going off over and over, making me rue my failure of putting on my DND. And it wasn't stopping, so there was no way to ignore the noise.

Instead of opening my eyes, I fumbled around the nightstand with my hand, leaving them covered. It must have been late since the entire room had gotten dark. Opening my bleary, tear-hazed eyes, I blinked a few times to adjust to the blinding light in the darkness.

There were several notifications in every platform, each letting me know I was tagged by... someone.

Lover_boi99 had posted something for me on each page, even the ones I'd blocked tagging on, which was weird.

I sat up, sure I was under a cyberattack, and blinked

hard to clear my vision. I tapped the first site notice and it opened onscreen. Thank goodness for facial recognition working in the dark since I certainly wouldn't have had the comprehension needed to enter my password.

The screen opened black at first, linking me to a video of... BTG. Must have been a promo for the fans. Yeah, it was hella late, but there was never not a good time to listen to BTG. Never.

I sat up and propped two pillows behind my head to see better and waited. Surely... there was some mistake. I hit the button to take it back to the beginning. And there it was again. My name was up in lights. And not just any name... *Gigi*. To be clear, it read *Gigi, I'm sorry*.

OMFG.

# CHAPTER 25

## CALEB GREENE

*S*urely, she'd seen the video. Hell, I watched it again from my seat at the second level bar at the Marriott in the middle of Times Square. Not only had I gotten a message to BTG, begging them to write a song, but I'd also contributed to their favorite cause in return for the favor. If I didn't stop all this philanthropy, I was going to be broke.

In each of those moments, the only thing I'd been thinking was none of it mattered if she saw me as a shitty person. Some rich guy who went around taking what he wanted without regard to anyone else's feelings. To be honest, I was that guy. But she'd opened my eyes to him. Whether it was eating burritos from a street vendor, giving money to the homeless, thinking of a colleague in a different light, or just taking the time to enjoy a song instead of focusing on what I wanted. What I needed. She made me see it all as worthwhile because it wasn't just about me.

The midnight release—BTG had thought of that one —made it possible to get the video played on the Times

Square Cams. The song, which they'd also written and recorded a video for, played on four of the giant screens. I watched as the lead singer, Kao, belted out the lyrics he'd texted me.

*If I'd known I was losing you from the very first day, I would have remembered your kiss.*

*If I'd understood you weren't mine, I would have spent more time trying to make you smile.*

*From the day I met you, you were all I needed. How can I make you see it's you I miss?*

*You're all I had, Gigi.*

*You're the one I need and want.*

*There's nothing I wouldn't do to have you by my side.*

*Nothing I wouldn't do to show you all of my love.*

*When I met you, you were an angel too special to hold.*

*One look from you and my world started to fold.*

*So I made myself a new person before your eyes.*

*Even if all the while, I knew you'd figure out my lies...*

*You're all I had, Gigi.*

*You're the one I need and want.*

*There's nothing I wouldn't do to have you by my side.*

*Nothing I wouldn't do to show you all of my love.*

*The day you walked out of my life, everything fell apart.*

*I can't eat, sleep, only lying awake in the dark.*

*I want you back, but understand.*

*There is no way I deserve to be your man.*


CONSIDERING ALL THE VIDEOS GIGI HAD MADE ME sit through, I couldn't believe how well-choreographed their moves were. They made a few hours' work look like child's play. The moment they'd sent me the link, I'd created a profile for the event on every single social media site and had uploaded the video just before the worldwide release, which was playing on screens in Tokyo, New York, and LA. It was a big deal.

But, hadn't it been necessary? She needed to know she was everything to me. Yet, as the world watched, I wondered if she'd even seen it. They'd blended in the pictures I'd sent of her with the background graphics, and even onscreen, she was breathtaking. How could I have been such a fucking fool?

It was my last play. A song meant to tell her the reason why I'd done what I'd done. Fluff leapt into my lap. I hadn't been able to bring myself to get rid of him. He was all I had left of her, after all.

When it was over, I stepped back into the upper lobby of the hotel and placed the glass that had held my cognac on one of the tables near the balcony. It was the perfect place to watch the display. The only thing that would have made it better would have been if she were at my side.

When my phone went off, I sent a silent prayer up that it was her. I pulled it from my sport jacket's interior pocket, almost cursing when it wasn't her. It was Dex. He'd either talked to Owenthal or seen the video. No way to tell which, but I already knew he was going to rag on me for both. "Yeah," I barked into the receiver.

"Shit, man. I thought you were going to put up a fight. You got knocked out without a punch."

Figures he was calling about the lawsuit. "Yeah, I know it was the right thing to do."

"Yeah, it was."

I was almost shocked. Dex was, at one point, one of the shrewdest businessmen around. This fact didn't necessarily lend itself to giving away a few million—*tens* of millions—to an ex-partner. Suffice to say, him agreeing with me was kind of confounding. "I don't ever like getting my ass raked over coals, but no matter how much money I had, it would have forever been a lie. I couldn't live with that anymore."

"Caleb, that was fucking decent. I know how worried you must be, but eventually, you'll get the money back. Your customers know you for quality and enjoy your product. Add on the decency for the cherry on top, and you're damn near a saint."

"I wouldn't say that, buddy. But thanks. Your support means everything."

When the line grew quiet, I glanced at the screen to see if he was still on.

"Dex?"

"Yup, I'm here. I was just wondering whether it was safe to ask you *the* question..."

"And what question might that be?"

"The one about the entire Square being lit up like a Christmas tree? That shit is all over the news. And serves as the other reason I'm calling. I wanted to make sure you hadn't fallen and cracked your skull open. This is extreme... even for you."

I had to smile, even if my heart was broken into shards. "It is. But I was wrong. I needed to do something big... And how'd you know it was me?"

"You've been moping around for days. And anytime someone asks you about what's going on, you change the subject or mention something about Geneva. Doesn't take a brain surgeon to—"

"Whatever, man. I'm doing okay. Maybe if I get to

explain to her in person, I'll tell her you think I have a concussion."

"She won't care. She loves you. You just need to let her see you love her too. And on that note, gotta go. The little princess is out of bed, so I'll have to go tuck her in. Be easy, man."

"Yeah. You too."

He was right. I just hoped my Gigi knew it.

# CHAPTER 26

## GENEVA CHAPMAN

*I* was crying again. I'd replayed the video so many times, but the tears wouldn't stop. The song, the words, the emotion... it meant everything to me. Trying to clear my throat and regain at least partial sight wasn't even the hardest part. I needed to call Caleb... the thought of him and the hurt I felt still juxtaposed with the sweetest thing anything had ever done for me.

He needed to know what this meant to me. I loved the music and even more, that it was being performed by BTG. And even bigger, I was in love with Caleb. Whether I wanted to admit it or not.

Yet, there were still boundaries that had been crossed. I picked up the phone to call him even if I didn't know what exactly to say. Another errant sniffle caught me just as he was answering the phone.

"Hello?" His voice was smooth. No crying for him.

That factoid only made me feel more self-conscious. "Hi. Um... I saw the video."

"And what did you think of it?"

"Well, given it's one a.m., it was very good. I'll reserve further comment until I've watched it another hundred or so times. I'm not even kidding."

"Yeah. Kao is a wonderful singer. I'll let him know you were pleased." The only sound on the other end was a long breath. I wasn't sure of the exact reason, but I hoped it was relief.

"Very." If I closed my eyes, I could hear the words prattling around in my mind. It was so incredibly beautiful. But I wasn't there to talk about the video. "Um, I need to see you because we have some things to discuss." I held my breath, waiting for the answer, even if he had asked for that originally. Just for me to sit and listen to his side of the story. I hadn't wanted to listen. I'd only wanted to make it go away. For *him* to go away.

"Yeah. Do you want me to send a car for you?"

"I could take you up on that. But you aren't horribly far, so I could easily walk."

"I'm not at the warehouse anymore." I almost heard the headshaking from the receiver. In another moment, I heard the phone get covered and some inaudible murmuring. "Okay. The driver will be there in about ten minutes."

"All right. I'll see you then."

Once we ended the call, I sought fresh loungewear, some nearly neutral makeup, and a hair tie to secure my curls. They were magnificent, but I didn't want to wear them down. I needed to be serious—we needed to talk about our future, or whatever was left of it—and my ringlets were serving "fun and carefree." I ended up in a purple T-shirt dress, and a matching slick of lipstick finished my natural-girl ensemble.

The driver took me to the hotel, and I walked into the lobby. Caleb could have easily just said the name. Everyone knew about the Marriott Marquis in Times Square. I just hated going there since there were so many tourists. Why hadn't he just stayed at the loft?

If I were being honest, the real reason I regretted our meeting was because I wouldn't know the outcome until we sat down and talked. I dreaded possibly running off the only man for whom I'd ever cared so deeply.

Instead of pondering that nightmare, I approached a guard on the street level of the hotel. "Hi, I'm looking for A Lounge?"

He looked up from his paper, his gray hair making that scenario work for him. "Sure, miss. Head over to that elevator bank and press level three, or you may take the escalators up, and they're just on the other side on your right."

"Okay... okay, thanks." I tried to steady myself as I followed the directions. I was nervous to see him. I just hoped we could find our way back.

One more deep breath and I was off. Sure, Caleb had been kind enough in apologizing, but I needed to be assured I could trust him. I needed to know he wouldn't do it again. I didn't even know the reason he'd lied, but he could have told me the truth long before now. Long before we'd taken it so far. I would have kept his secrets, if that was what it was all about.

I headed to the escalator, and instead of my normal gauntlet-style run up to the floor, I waited patiently for the slow-moving stairs to take me where I needed to be. The entire way up, I thought about what I would say. Funny how you're supposed to know those things with someone you had fallen for, but every time I considered how the conversation would go, I seized up.

I stepped off, bracing myself for laying eyes on him. He was my weakness, and seeing him was only going to amplify the desire.

But when I rounded the corner to reach the bar, I thought I was in the wrong place. The restaurant was decorated in all white, everything from the tablecloths to centerpieces spilling over with white flowers from hydrangea to lilacs to gerbera daisies. Even the twinkling lights all around the room that accented the windows overlooking Times Square were white. I nearly stepped back until I saw what I was looking for. Caleb.

He was dressed in an all-white suit, his hand in one pocket, the other wrapped around a glass of some type of liquor. Heat ran up my entire person, and I knew I was in trouble. No way would I be able to control the conversation.

"Geneva, welcome." As he spoke to me, the song... *my* song piped into the restaurant, filling the space with his apology. My heart fluttered. I used to think people were making that sensation up, but no. It was real. He was real. "I'm Caleb. It is very nice to meet you."

He sauntered over to me, exuding confidence and—somehow, at the same time—remorse. The scent of some-thing lovely came with him. He was all sandalwood and whiskey. Decadent and fine as hell.

"Hello," I said. It was the only thing I had. Later, I would look back and wish I'd been more eloquent, had said something momentous. But at the moment, hello was a feat.

"Please, join me." He reached for my hand, and when I gave it to him, he slightly turned, leading me across the restaurant to a table lit with tall, tapered candles and a long centerpiece.

I would have been self-conscious in my T-shirt dress, but there was no one else there. "Where is everyone?" I glanced around the room before taking the seat he pulled out for me.

"I have a friend who owed me a favor." He walked around me and sat in the chair opposite me at the table.

"Oh…" Again, I was at a loss.

"I wanted to tell you something. I was about to reach out to you right before you called. I needed you to come and get to know the real me. I'm afraid it's been far too long, and you might walk out of my life. And what would I tell Fluff?"

I tried to block the smile threatening to betray the take-no-shit-woman persona I wanted to rock. Not sure it worked, but I went on. "I wouldn't be walking away if it weren't for your actions, Caleb." I still hadn't managed to say his real name without it being tipped in ice. I took a sip of the water immediately after because my throat was dry as the Sahara.

"I know. None of this is on you. It's all on me. But when I saw you the first time, I was so ashamed of who I was, even if I didn't realize it at the time. I didn't want you to know the real me. It was nice to have someone look at me and see me for who I was. I know I lied about my name. But that is all I lied about. I wasn't born rich. I had to work my way up to where I am now. And if it weren't for you, I wouldn't have even realized how much of a dick I'd become." Caleb sighed and leaned back into his chair, looking away, then returned his attention to me. He finally settled on resting his elbows on the table. "Do you believe in fate?"

"I guess. I mean, I've had some pretty tough breaks, so it's hard to believe in something you can't see." And there it was. For a fleeting moment, I didn't feel the stab of pain for everything I'd lost. It boiled down to one simple question. Why should I trust him?

# CHAPTER 27

## CALEB GREENE

*W*hat could I say or do to help her forgive me? I'd known earlier I wasn't leaving without giving us at least one more try. This was it. It would be my last chance to convince her. She was everything to me. I wasn't even sure how it had happened in such a short time, but there I was. As I stared across the table at her, I realized she was probably in the most relaxed clothes and the least amount of makeup I'd seen her in, and she was still the most beautiful thing in my entire lifetime. "I know. Life doesn't give us a lot of support in the faith area. But, when I met you, something in me let me know you were my destiny. Even if I wasn't ready for you yet." Sure, it sounded campy, but I was telling her the truth. If she would give me one more chance, I would never, ever lie to her again.

"I knew... well, at the time, I thought you were special too. And then we spent so much time together. I really enjoyed it. I thought I was finally on a good path. With getting the job offer from Montague, meeting you, and oh, let's not forget, my sister's app was approved for start-up cash." With that, she leaned back in her seat and leveled a suspicious glare at me.

"That's great. Should I... should I know something about that?" I had to ask because, with each passing second, her normally big brown eyes were narrowing to slits.

"Well... the award came from AppTech. I would be a fool not to think you had something to do with it." She leaned away from the table, and I could almost feel the distance she put between us.

"No, I didn't know she was applying. Hell, I didn't even know it was time to begin submissions. I've been a little checked out. One thing I've learned, though. If your sister is anything like you, she earned the grant. I'm just glad my company is the one to give it to her." I probably shouldn't have been smiling, but honestly, I was impressed.

"So, even when I told you she was taking it out to VC firms, you thought nothing about your own company?" Now she was leaning forward onto the table, her elegant fingers interlocked over the place setting.

"No." I leaned forward too and looked directly into her eyes. I wanted her to know I wasn't making shit up. I wanted her to feel me. "I was so caught up in the lawsuit, there was nothing breaking through that agony. Until..." I held my head down in an effort to avoid her glare but recovered quickly. I had to press on. Even if she ended up hating me. "Until the day I met you, nothing else could force me to pay attention, to pull my head out of my ass. Then, there you were."

"Tell me why you lied, Caleb. You at least owe me that." She rested her arms on the table and matched my intensity.

"Well, when I met you, you just assumed I was Mac. I saw it as an opportunity to get to know you a little and to allow me to easily free myself from the situation after I was done with the case. But then, I got to know you. And the truth is, I was ready to tell you so many times. I just didn't want you to leave me or lose respect for me. I was a coward. I wasn't the man you deserve. I should have been, because you gave me every opportunity to."

She took another sip of her water like a predator waiting to land the killing blow. Her eyes had softened, though, the warm brown filled with candlelight. After she put the glass back on the table, she returned her attention to me. "Okay, so now is your chance. Tell me, why should I overlook this, and how will I know you won't do it again?"

"Okay. So—" I took a deep breath before launching into what I hoped would be a game-changing argument on the pro side of things. Funny, I hadn't been nearly as nervous during the mediation as I was seated before this breathtaking woman. I had been a goner from the moment I laid eyes on her, and tonight was no exception. "I should have told you who I was. No excuse for that action. But every moment after, I was myself. I honestly was into our group project. I do hate eating from food trucks, but I was pleasantly surprised by the ones you took me to. My favorite pastime is coding, as sad as that is. And I do love the way you look when you laugh. I lied about my name, but it didn't matter... because... because I'd already given you my heart. And I would do absolutely anything for you." I ran my hands over my hair and leaned away. Those were the most real words I'd ever said to anyone. But she deserved the truth.

She sat there, running a finger around the rim of her

glass. I prayed she wasn't about to throw it in my face and storm out of there. Then I caught the hint of a smile starting in the corner of her mouth. "And... how about the future? Caleb Greene, would you ever lie to me again?"

I couldn't help the smile I gave her. "Only about your cooking. But if it's bad, we can get some couples cooking courses."

Something I thought I would never see again happened in the next few seconds. She smiled and her shoulders dropped, the defensiveness easing from her face. "Well... I think you'd better always tell me my food tastes delicious. So, I guess I can forgive you that one tiny, tiny malfeasance."

"Then, you do forgive me?"

"Caleb, to be honest, I forgave you when BTG wrote that song for me. I wasn't ready to say it aloud, but yes. I forgive you and will never again refuse to hear your side of things. I mean, we'll argue one day again, but we'll have to work on the listening part."

"I can't tell you how my heart was jackhammering in my chest. I thought you were going to walk out of here. Walk out of my life. For good."

"Well, you should come over here and kiss me before I change my mind."

I couldn't say anything to Geneva while every part of me screamed to take her. To kiss her sweet lips, to taste her essence, to revel in her kindness and beauty. I stood and walked to her side of the table before sliding my hand behind her neck to tilt her head up, leaning in to press our lips together. As the heat took hold, I slid in deeper, my tongue probing the sweetness of her mouth. Her body strained as she made an effort to meet my kisses.

In one motion, I lowered to one knee before her,

bringing her succulent lips to mine once again. My fingers caressed her back, and I wished I could feel her skin. I moved down her back to the softness of her ass. I played at the hem of her dress, running a hand beneath it to feel the silkiness of her panties. A moan released in my mouth, and I replied by pressing into the soft cleft at her core.

She responded to me by rocking forward onto my hand, my circular motion against the silky panties bringing her to a shudder. I could almost taste her.

"Um... I can come back," I heard from behind me. The waitress. Dammit to hell. Gigi was of no use, either, as her head was tilted back, giving me full access to her body. The whole in-public thing had failed to register to either of us.

"Oh, just one second, if you don't mind?" I blocked Gigi from sight as she adjusted her dress and underwear.

"Sure, Mr. Greene. I'll be right back in a few moments." And she was gone.

"Thanks."

On the recovery, Gigi sat up and let out a giggle. "Oh my God, can you even imagine? We were almost exhibitionists."

I had to laugh along with her. "I don't think that was included in the deal I got when I booked the restaurant." My body grew cold as soon as I moved away from her, her warmth too much to leave behind.

"I don't think that counted as exhibitionism." Gigi shifted in her seat and pulled the chair to the table, probably to keep me from going after her again.

"What do you say we get out of here the second we're done eating? Or did you want more groveling?" I hadn't really wanted to ask, but my dick was pressing against the zipper of the tailored slacks in the worst way. If I didn't leave soon, I was going to be in real trouble. Every part of me wanted inside her.

"Not so fast. I never got to address my part in all of this."

I knew where she was headed. I'd said some pretty shitty things to her in the heat of the moment. "I really didn't mean all those th—"

"I was wrong. I blamed you for a lot of things related to my mom and dad's relationship. Even from the start, I... I guess I was just waiting for you to hurt me. Like every other man. I spent so many years upset because my mother's need to be rescued allowed her to put up with so many of my father's bad habits. It wasn't her fault that she fell in love with him. And while it was unrealistic, I went through every relationship punishing men because of him. And that was my own fault. Feeling like that left me vulnerable, even when I'd intended the opposite effect. I built some pretty high walls around my heart. And when you didn't tell me who you were, I was ready to cut and run. What I didn't realize was I had cut and run from the start. For that, I'm sorry."

I didn't stop her, letting her get all that out. I watched as she fidgeted through something so hard to acknowledge —our own bad actions. Honestly, she didn't have shit on me. I wasn't even made, but I wouldn't take that away from her too. If she wanted to talk all night, I would listen. For her, I was all in. "It's understandable for you to be wary of men when the whole of us aren't always good to people who are good to us. This isn't your fault. I accept your apology, though. And I want you to know, I will never purposefully hurt you again. We both can learn from the past."

A warm smile spread over her lips. I just stared at her,

my own angel on earth. She was breathtaking when she was happy. If I had to spend the rest of my life to get that smile again, so be it. "See, I can grow too. Now, let's order some food so we can go back to my place and spend the rest of the night making up with one another."

"That ain't a problem. Not in the least bit." I waved my hand to the server who had been so patiently waiting until I summoned her. All the while knowing I was truly the luckiest man alive.

# CHAPTER 28

## GENEVA CHAPMAN

*L*eddie was already in bed when we arrived. And while Caleb had suggested we go to the hotel where he was actually staying, I didn't believe I was ready to step into his multimillionaire world just yet. Besides, it had been nice to look across and see BTG serenading me on the cams in Times Square. My pictures were even included in the video for all the world to see. I flipped on the light as we crossed over the threshold of my boudoir.

"I love your bedroom. It reminds me of high school." Caleb whispered the words into my hair from his position behind me. From the moment we walked into my apartment, he'd been hot on my heels, arms locked around my waist, and penguin stepping in unison with me.

"Oh, my high school bedroom was much messier." I laughed. I should have cleaned it at some point, but I'd spent the last eight days faceplanted on my bed. I quickly ran around the bed, picked up all the wads of tissue left over from my crying spells and threw them into the trash. When I was done, Caleb fell onto the bed, crossed his legs, and watched as I hung up random clothes and took my shoes into the closet. He smiled as I turned back to him. "You know, I'm probably killing the mood."

"Nonsense. You keep bending over. I find that sexy as fuck."

"Sexy A-F, huh? Wait 'til you see me clean the bathroom."

"You can do whatever you want, but I will never lose interest in watching you. Even if you were cleaning an elephant's ass. I'd still be horny."

"Now that is troubling."

"Try me. We can rent out the zoo right now."

Pulling my dress over my head, I was both thankful that I wore a pretty bra and panties, and also that I hadn't turned the lights off. For the first time, I wanted someone to see me. I wanted *Caleb* to see me. "I don't think we want to go to the zoo right now, do we?" I dropped the dress to the floor. His eyes roved over my body, and I tried my hardest to push my insecurities from my mind.

"Hell no. Nothing could tear me from this spot." Caleb licked his full lips and stood from the bed. In what seemed like seconds, he had his shoes, pants, and jacket off, and his shirt open, revealing his pecs and dangerous abs. The bulge in his boxers was massive, and my mouth went dry as he stalked toward me, then wrapped me in an embrace.

I sank into him, inhaling his clean, masculine scent. The heat from his body contradicted the chill that ran over my flesh as his hands went to my hair to gently remove the band that held it in place. He tousled my curls, running his fingers through the strands. No one else was permitted to be so intimate with me. "You are so goddamn beautiful, Geneva."

I thought at once to say something clever, but I lost the battle when his mouth claimed my own, at first soft and probing, then more intense, exploring. He demanded everything I could give to him in the moment, and I melted, the heat of my core blending with the erratic rhythm of my heart. I was his. Every single part of me.

Raising my legs to wrap around his waist, I felt the friction of his erection against my sex as he carried me to my bed. I ached for him to be inside me. He lay me on my back, only breaking our kiss to unclasp my bra and slide my panties off my legs. He stared at my bared body, his heavy-lidded eyes leaving tangible trails of warmth as his gaze passed over every inch of me. I was so turned on, my wet pussy pulsed like a second heartbeat between my slick thighs.

He removed his shirt, then his boxers. My mouth grew dry, and I savored his bare chest, his muscled shoulders, his everything. I wanted him inside me but didn't want to rush the moment. I wanted to savor it. When he was done, he pulled a condom from his pocket, and the soft crackle of the wrapper being removed filled the weighted silence between us. I watched as he rolled it over his shaft. Consumed with desire, I ran a hand down my body and held his gaze as I spread my legs and dipped a finger deep inside of me. We both moaned, and I didn't know whose was louder, hungrier.

Caleb sank to his knees, wrapped his hands around my thighs, and pulled me down the bed until my body was immediately in front of his mouth. I could feel the heat of his breath on my flesh, and I whispered, "Caleb, take me."

He was on me before I could finish the demand, his tongue playing with my clit. His fingers caressed my sex, and I came undone. I gripped at the comforter in some inane effort to keep me on the planet, gently rocking my hips against his face, practically vibrating with sexual energy as his beard and chin delivered the needed extra sensation.

"This is mine," he growled, breaking the connection between my flesh and his for the first time in a while.

"Oh, yes..." I was shattering into a million pieces and being put back together again, but I had to acknowledge his claim to my body. The claiming of my heart. With one last undulation of his tongue against my sex, my release took hold and caused me to quake with pleasure. I cried out, hoping I wasn't disturbing the neighbors. Hell, I hoped I wasn't disturbing the Martians. My thighs tightened around his neck, pressing him into me as I rode out the erotic waves of our passion.

"Fuck, Caleb." My legs went lax on his shoulders, and I drew in a shuddering breath, praying it would bring me back to earth and soothe the out-of-body experience I was currently undergoing. I was thoroughly spent, but he pressed one last kiss on my clit and rose to his full height once he was done ravishing me.

"Ready for more?"

~

## CALEB GREENE

I could have stayed in her sweetness forever, but my shaft ached for her.

"Yessss..." Her voice was a lazy growl, uninhibited and sexy. I stared down at her—the curves of her body slicked with sweat, her lipstick ruined, her fluffy curls sprawled around her head—and I wanted more.

Words escaped me as I leaned down on top of her and took her mouth, carefully balancing my weight on my elbows so I didn't crush her. It was too good. I could have orgasmed right in that moment, but I fought the urge and broke off our kiss. I moved to her ear and whispered, "I love you, Geneva," before I kissed my way down her neck to suckle her breast. Her legs wrapped around my waist, heels sinking into my back, her body urging me inside her.

"I love you too, Caleb. And I want you inside me now."

"I want to take my time with you..."

"I get it, but don't tease me. I can't take it."

I laughed against her breast before positioning myself at her entrance and slowly moving inside her tightness. Her hiss of pleasure made me tease at her nipple with my teeth, and she shuddered beneath me. I filed yet another way to pleasure her into my memory. Geneva was everything I wanted, and I would spend the rest of my life trying to please her.

I pulled out, entering her in a rush, her moans urging me on, demanding everything I could give her. I wanted to worship her in every way. Faster, and her legs quaked on my waist. Again, I dove in deep and welcomed the fluttering of her pussy. The heat of her body was enough to make me lose it, but I wanted to be there for a while—inside her, my life just beginning.

This woman was my undoing, the key to my heart and the stars to my moon.

"It's so good..." she cried out.

I had to stare at her for a minute. Her eyes were squeezed shut, and my name on her kiss-swollen lips urged me to go deeper, harder. I was lost in her. She bit her lip and released a moan that almost sounded lyrical, as if I were the bass and she were the treble.

All I could do was moan my agreement. It took every ounce of strength to keep from crumbling around her. I was a mere breath away from her capturing my soul. She put her arms around my neck and pulled me close—her turn to draw me into a passionate kiss. She suckled my tongue, the sensation making me weak as erotic surges laid waste to me. In order to anchor myself, I wrapped my arms around her. The bed rocked as my pace intensified, the headboard creaking from the back-and-forth motion and the demands of our writhing bodies.

I was in her—mind, body, and soul—and nothing in the world could make me leave this woman. I pulled away from her mouth to retain control and to draw in a desperately needed breath before kissing her over her neck and shoulders.

I pressed a forefinger into her mouth as I grasped her neck, allowing her to suckle the digit with all the magnificence of that marvelous opening.

"Geneva... Geneva..." I wasn't even sure why I was calling her name, but somehow, it slowed the tsunami inside me that threatened to overtake me.

Her teeth scraped against the tip of my finger as I watched her, and it was all I could take. I shuddered and struggled for some semblance of control as I moved inside her, her core wet for me, her body grasping my cock.

A blast of heat broke over my body, quickly replaced by the coolness of release as I came. My calves spasmed while my body tensed and, for a moment, all I could see were stars. I cried out her name again, and at once, she stiffened in my arms, her sex milking what remained from me.

As much as I wanted to stay inside her, to lie in her arms until the sun fell from the sky, I rolled onto my back and pulled her limp body onto mine. "Gigi, I think you're going to kill me." I kissed her on top of her head, her curls soft against my lips.

"I could easily say the same for you. I never wanted you to stop. Although, at some point, we'll probably need food, have to go to work, whatever. None of that seems to matter when I'm with you."

"I know. I'm pretty sure you could tell me to stay here forever, and I would. So, please don't do that. One of us has to have a level head."

She giggled, and I felt her body shake beneath me. Her soft breasts against my chest had me semi-hard again, and the only thing keeping me from taking her again was the lack of another condom. Damn, I wanted her. Nothing in my life had ever been so good. Not just the sex, but *her*. Geneva had been everything I needed. I thought I'd had it all before meeting her, and now I knew I'd never truly been complete. Not in the most real way, the most important way. When it happened, though, I had welcomed it, whether I had wanted to acknowledge it or not.

After who knew how long, she lifted her head from my chest and rested her chin on her hand. Sleepy brown eyes stared back at me. "I'm going to go to the bathroom, then grab us some water. I'll bring you a towel... or we could shower together?"

"Door number two, please." Preempting her getaway, I gathered her up into one last epic kiss. Before I realized what was happening, my hand was on her sex again, her heat and wetness welcoming me inside once more.

"Whew, baby. Slow down. You know we need some water before we dehydrate in here." She laughed.

"You're probably right." I had to agree. I honestly couldn't feel my legs.

"I know I am. I'll be right back."

I couldn't help but watch as she rose from the bed; her lithe body in motion made me ache for her again. Like a good boy, I stayed put, even if it went against every instinct.

Once she was done in the en suite bath, she went and got us much-needed water. I greedily drank it down, hoping she would be ready for our shower. When she was, my cock nearly cheered. Thank fuck the asshole only had one eye and no mouth, or he would have been screaming too.

I was ready to spend the rest of my life with her. It was past time I let her know that.

# EPILOGUE

## GENEVA CHAPMAN

ONE YEAR LATER

"Hello!" I could hear Leddie screaming across the apartment. Our doorman, Michael, usually let her in whenever she arrived. I thought he had a crush on her, but I wouldn't dare snoop.

I ran out of the bedroom, careful of my too-big-for-first-trimester belly and happy my sister had stopped by, as usual. The allergy shots she started all on her own made it possible for both her and Fluff to be in my life simultaneously. Along with Caleb, of course.

"Hey there," I called out before swooping in and giving her a hug. Now that we didn't live together anymore, I was overly emotional each time I saw her. "Like the work we've done so far?" We were in the original loft I'd met Caleb in. God, I would have never thought we would be here given that I'd almost not accepted his apology.

"Love it. It's a neutral, but I actually like that. It suits y'all. All right, take me to the nursery where I'll spend hours with my niece or nephew."

"Oh, I thought you'd never ask. You know, Caleb painted this himself." I led the way down the giant hallway we'd expanded in width in case Leddie ever wanted to spend the weekend with us. It had only made sense since she and Caleb often worked on apps together.

"Oh, Lord. I'm surprised there's not paint all over the floors. You know he's not detail-oriented."

"I heard that, Leddie. Since I'm your new boss, you should watch it, smarty pants." Caleb barreled into the room, undoubtedly proud of his craftsmanship. "I put the crib together too."

"You know, you make enough money to hire people for that."

"I do, but your sister won't even let me take cabs. I'm saying she's a bit frugal, in case you missed that."

"Oh, don't I know it. She probably would have moved everyone into our apartment if she could have gotten away with it. And I'm just glad she cleaned her room before she left," Leddie joined in.

"I'm literally right here."

"Oh, my bad." Caleb guffawed. "Well, ladies, I'm gonna leave you to it. Dex is expecting me for some racquetball. If you need anything text me, okay, baby?" He leaned down and planted a kiss on me, something I never quite got enough of.

He opened his mouth and slipped his tongue inside, teasing me by withdrawing quickly. I knew it was to save Leddie from seeing us make out again. And while I understood it, it didn't stop me from yearning for his touch. Like always.

"I will," I said, once I caught my breath.

"All right," he said, giving me one last squeeze before releasing me. "And Leddie, I saw the new app lineup you sent over. I don't know about that one with the paper dolls..."

"*Glamourize.* Trust me. The women will eat it up. And since eighty-four percent of our market identifies as female, we need this added. We can talk more on Monday. Right now, I'm about to get elbow deep in baby clothes." Leddie rubbed her hands together and rolled over to the bags filled to bursting with tiny little gender-neutral clothes.

"Fine, fine. I'm gonna get out before y'all either kick me out or put me to work."

"There's always something to do. Just come on back if you get tired of Dex kicking your butt at racquetball."

I just watched as they went back and forth for several minutes. I didn't believe Leddie would ever get enough of teasing Caleb. She'd nearly kicked his ass herself, but eventually, they'd seemed to settle into a groove. Once she'd threatened his life if he ever hurt me again, that is.

"All right, girl, you win," Caleb finally said, tossing up the imaginary white flag. "I'm out. I'll let you know if I stop to pick up food."

"Thank you," I said.

"And Gigi..."

"Yup," I said, picking up a tiny T-shirt from the bag and folding it.

"*Nothing I wouldn't do to show you all of my love.*"

And that was it, I melted... again. Every time he quoted the song to me, I did the same thing. "I love you too, Caleb."

"Get a room," Leddie chimed in. I glanced over at her as she cradled the bundle of black fur in her arms.

Despite her not being a cat person, she and Fluff seemed right at home together.

This day, just like every day, made all of it worth it. And if I could do it all again, there's nothing I would change about falling for my irresistible intern.

## THE END

Want to keep up with all of the new releases in Vi Keeland and Penelope Ward's Cocky Hero Club world? Make sure you sign up for the official Cocky Hero Club newsletter for all the latest on our upcoming books: https://www.subscribepage.com/CockyHeroClub Check out other books in the Cocky Hero Club series: http://www.cockyheroclub.com

# ACKNOWLEDGMENTS

Oh my gosh, 2020! Amirite?? It was a year I will always remember. There was so much loss, devastation, and sadness in every pocket, every corner of the world. This book was the only thing I had to cling to outside of my family and a few close friends. I would peck at it and get out as many words as I could, when I could. Whether five or six showed up on the page or a thousand and six, I was grateful to have some life preserver to cling to as everything was thrown at each of us. I am so very happy to have completed this work to present to you all. It is my survival gift to every reader, fan, and blogger who made it to this page.

My family – Ryan, Keisha, Justin, Brandon, Brenna – thanks for dealing with my special branded of quirkiness. I don't know many who would be so willing. Everything I do, I do for you.

To Amalie, MK, Shaila, Sienna, and Sage – in alphabetical order because I could never place your names in order of importance. You mean too much to me and fill my heart every day. You all are a beacon of light in the darkness. We made it through Hell Year together and many hours of drinking via Zoom calls later, we are still standing. I value, trust, and believe in you more than you will ever know.

There are so many professionals who had patience through my writing drought and still reminded me that *I could* do it. Sara Megibow, my agent-extraordinaire, you are the real rock star. Also, the people who make up Cocky Hero Club, I appreciate your understanding and kindness immensely.

There are a few people who were integral to its creation and helped me wipe away all the mess to make it shine. There was Kate Marope who was the first editor, always there to chat and guide. Then, Jennifer Miller gave me so much to think about, to add, to reimagine. Thanks to you both for those hours of editing. I wouldn't be here without you. To A.J. at DeliciousNightsDesign.com, you are a world-class artist. Thank you.

I should stop now, but please know if you are reading this, I appreciate you most of all for trusting me with your entertainment and for sticking with Caleb, Geneva, and me until the words 'The End'. You are all the tops to me.

Always Shine Bright,

—Aliza

## AUTHOR BIO

Aliza has only ever wanted to write. Throughout her professional career in healthcare, raising two children, and eating her weight in chocolate, she never deviated from her dreams of one day, adding the notch of novelist to her belt. Author of paranormal and contemporary novels with their strong, quirky heroines in common, she continues to write the love stories of her heart. And perhaps, still eats just a little too much chocolate.

For more by Aliza Mann, visit her website at www.alizamannauthor.com.